Praise for S

"Loss, temporary and permanent, physical and emotional, is the hard, gleaming thread tying together Laken's short-story collection. . . . An absorbing literary exploration of the geography of loss."

—*Kirkus Reviews*

"Laken demonstrates that all of us are in some way isolated from others, trapped in our own thoughts, our own hurts, our own bodies. In setting her stories alternately in Russia and the United States, Laken shows that borders and oceans create less of a gulf than does the tiny space between two people. Bridging that chasm is our greatest challenge."

—*Booklist*

"Vivid and evocative, these stories will appeal to readers of both popular and literary fiction."

—*Library Journal*

"Valerie Laken proves herself again to be a writer of vast compassion, and dead-on accuracy, in these stories. *Separate Kingdoms* is a travel through the human psyche, but it is so rawly full of vivid places and pitch-perfect dialogue and sensory detail that you know you are in the visceral world of the characters as well as their minds. There are only eight stories here, but each one is so rich, so textured and nuanced, that I felt I'd dwelled among these familiar strangers in their kingdoms for a sumptuous period of years, and yet I started the collection again as soon as I had finished it, recalling things I felt an urgent need to

APR 07 2011

read again. Valerie Laken takes aim at the human experience, and does not shoot. Instead, she steps forward, into places we wouldn't dare, and lays them bare for the reader. This is life-changing work, the kind of reading one longs for and so rarely finds."
—Laura Kasischke, author of *In a Perfect World*

"Valerie Laken writes about the emotionally and physically maimed with a startling poignancy. Blind Russians, handicapped golfers, college exchange students, seizure victims: Laken can do it all. *Separate Kingdoms* is, quite simply, a wonderful collection."
—Joshua Henkin, author of *Matrimony*

"Beyond the luminous prose, the shining intelligence (as opposed to mere cleverness) and narrative boldness, what I perhaps prize most in Valerie Laken's work is an empathy that knows no boundaries. She conjures her disparate figures and settings with a clear-eyed authenticity that goes beyond mere detail, arrowing in on the emotional truth of a character or situation."
—Peter Ho Davies, author of *The Welsh Girl*

"This is a pitch-perfect collection, searching and graceful, containing just the right mixture of intelligence and heart. The separate kingdoms Valerie Laken writes about are not only America and Russia, the countries where her stories take place, but also the innermost minds of any two human beings, and the different ways we experience the world before and after a catastrophe. All of the characters in this book are missing something deeply important to them—children or pets, spells of time or pieces of their own bodies. In Laken's skillful and compassionate hands, though, they are never less than whole."

—Kevin Brockmeier, author of *The Brief History of the Dead*

"What I find so striking about this book is the way that separate worlds—seemingly foreign or even bizarre to each other—are brought together and forced to converse, to try to love each other. There is considerable erotic energy in such a meeting. The imagination in these stories often does what it can to heal a wound or a rift, and so the stories often have an amazing poignancy that never lapses into the maudlin."

—Charles Baxter, author of
the National Book Award finalist *The Feast of Love*

"A work of daunting versatility and technical skill, the product of a writer absolutely at home in the language and working vigorously within both new and old forms. . . . This is a writer of wonderful gifts."

—Michael Byers, author of *Long for this World*

ALSO BY VALERIE LAKEN

• • •

Dream House

stories

Valerie Laken

NEW YORK • LONDON • TORONTO • SYDNEY • NEW DELHI • AUCKLAND

HARPER PERENNIAL

The following stories have appeared in somewhat different forms in the following publications: "Before Long" in *Ploughshares* and the *Pushcart Prize XVIII*; "Spectators" in *Ploughshares*; "Family Planning" in the *Missouri Review*; "Remedies" in *Meridian*; "God of Fire" in *Michigan Quarterly Review*; and "Separate Kingdoms" in *Alaska Quarterly Review*.

P.S.™ is a trademark of HarperCollins Publishers.

SEPARATE KINGDOMS. Copyright © 2011 by Valerie Laken. All rights reserved. Printed in the United States of America. No part of this book may be used or reproduced in any manner whatsoever without written permission except in the case of brief quotations embodied in critical articles and reviews. For information address HarperCollins Publishers, 10 East 53rd Street, New York, NY 10022.

HarperCollins books may be purchased for educational, business, or sales promotional use. For information please write: Special Markets Department, HarperCollins Publishers, 10 East 53rd Street, New York, NY 10022.

FIRST EDITION

Designed by Cassandra J. Pappas

Library of Congress Cataloging-in-Publication Data
Laken, Valerie.
Separate kingdoms : stories / by Valerie Laken. — 1st ed.
p. cm.
ISBN 978-0-06-084094-5 (pbk.)
1. United States—Social life and customs—Fiction. I. Title.
PS3612.A535S47 2011
813'.6—dc22
2010034615

11 12 13 14 15 OV/RRD 10 9 8 7 6 5 4 3 2 1

Once they left me alone I decided to occupy myself with the affairs of state. I discovered that Spain and China are one and the same country, and it is only through ignorance that they are considered to be separate kingdoms. I recommend everyone try to write Spain on a bit of paper and see, it will always turn out China.

—Nikolai Vasilievich Gogol, "Diary of a Madman"

• • •

Being who you are is not a disorder.

—Franz Wright, "Pediatric Suicide"
from *Wheeling Motel* (Knopf, 2009)

CONTENTS

• • •

BEFORE LONG

IN THE DAYS that summer when his mother had to work cleaning the cottages in Drezna and Rudino, Anton was being watched by the Shurins. He was twelve and blind, and his mother feared leaving him alone. In the mornings he worked with Oleg Shurin in the tomato patches along the bluff, and when they finished they took long walks on the dirt paths of the fields and forests around their village. Anton would follow Oleg's voice or the crackle of his steps through the grass and do his best to map their course in his mind, counting paces and turns, charting sounds and directions and angles of descent or ascent. Beyond the tomato patches and the bluff was a deep ravine leading down to the river, which ran shallow and calm that year because of the drought.

They had finished watering the plants, and the sun was high but there was still time before lunch, so Anton and Oleg were down in the ravine near a clump of bushes where Oleg kept his magazines hidden in a metal box. Oleg was three years older and was teaching Anton about women. He had seen and touched and kissed them. The two of them lay in the weedy undergrowth and Oleg described the pictures.

"—on her knees with her hand down against—"

"Wait, where?"

"There." Oleg took Anton's finger and touched it to the flimsy paper, tracing out a vague pattern. "Her crotch, like."

"She's naked?"

"She has a scarf. An orange scarf, thin, kind of twisted around her."

"Like a snake?"

"No, you idiot." Oleg sighed. "Well, OK, sort of like a snake."

Anton lay back again in the dry, scratchy grass, feeling gravity pull harder as he relaxed. He trailed a few fingers from his neck down to his breastplate. Along the ridges of his rib cage to his stomach and hip.

"And then what?" he said.

"That's all." Oleg rustled the magazines back into their box.

"Wait. What issue is it?"

"May 1991."

Two years old. Oleg got them used for cheap. "What about her legs? What kind of legs?"

"We're done, Anton. Go on." The metal box clicked shut. "Go on, go."

Anton got up and walked down toward the river to give Oleg his privacy. He slipped off his sandals and felt his way down the bank with his hands close to the ground, then waded several steps into the water. It was only knee-deep this summer, but still he was forbidden to go near it.

He stood up to his calves and felt the water swerve in circles around his feet. Something soft, a leaf maybe, drifted between his legs. The tug and push of the water affirmed his bearings. He was still facing east, still perpendicular to the bank. He turned downstream, unzipped his pants, and relieved himself.

"Zzzzzzz," Oleg called from the ravine when he was finished. That was the sound of Dr. Nicholson's drill. Anton made his way out of the water. From across the river he could hear hammers striking and echoing where workers were building more summer cottages for the New Russians from Moscow, who weren't Communists.

"He's going to rip them right out. Pop!" Oleg splashed some water at him.

Anton was going to the dentist tomorrow. Neither of them had ever been, but a year ago Anton's mother had started cleaning house for an American dentist, Dr. Nicholson, and he was giving them a special rate. Anton felt for his sandals along the bank where he had left them.

"Looking for these?" Oleg tapped him on the head with the sandals.

"Give me them."

"Just *kidding*." Oleg put the sandals into his hand.

Anton tried to clear the distress from his face. "I know." Oleg was only teaching him to be tough.

"Got something for you." Oleg pressed some bills into Anton's palm. "Tomorrow, if you get a chance, see if you can get me a copy of *Pentxaus.* My cousin says he finds them in the metro."

Anton shuffled the bills through his fingers. "Well. I won't be alone, you know?"

"Ah, of course. Your mother by your side. I can see how that poses a problem." Oleg had started talking this way lately. He was getting ready for tenth grade.

"Not that I don't want to." Anton held out the rubles for him to take back.

"Of course." Oleg started up the ravine. "Me, if I were going, it'd be a different situation."

Oleg's grandmother called for them from the top of the bluff.

Anton fastened the last buckle of his sandals and hurried after him. "Maybe you could come with us."

"To the American sadist? No thanks."

Anton pushed the fistful of bills at Oleg's back. "Ah, just keep the money," Oleg said. "In case. Just see what you can do."

"I could buy some gum for you."

"And some *candies*?" Oleg said in a little girl's voice.

"Maybe your mom will run off to the bathroom," Oleg said after a while. "Leave you waiting next to a newsstand."

Anton turned the idea over in his mind. It could happen.

"Maybe some girl will pick you up at the station, show you something."

Anton could feel his face starting to flush. "Maybe Dr. Nicholson has a nurse."

"Exactly. She's going to lean all over you. Because you're so irresistible."

They were halfway up the ravine by now. "Wait." Oleg turned suddenly and grabbed him by the shoulders. Anton steadied himself and took a breath. "This secret dies with me," Oleg chanted three times, spinning him around and around on the uneven soil. Then they stood still, waiting for the dizziness to subside, and Anton repeated the chant himself. It was an empty ritual left over from the days before they'd really become friends. Who would he tell? Why? No one had ever shown him as much as Oleg had.

The spinning had no effect anymore anyway. Anton was pretty sure he could make his way to Oleg's secret stash alone, in the rain, even in the snow, if he wanted. It was sixty-five paces west of the railway bridge, and with the noise of the stream as a guide there was almost no way to get lost. Anton had memorized the entire village by following in Oleg's footsteps. Now he scrambled up the ravine in the path Oleg snapped through the brush, keeping low to the ground and using his hands for balance.

"Where have you been?" Oleg's grandmother approached them after they crossed the field and neared her house. She jingled a little for some reason as she walked.

"We caught that rabbit eating at the plants again," Oleg said. "We were chasing it down."

"My boys. Did you catch it?"

Oleg nudged him. "Not yet. Maybe after lunch."

Oleg's grandmother put a hand on Anton's back and patted it. "I bet you'll get it next time. Can you catch a rabbit, Anton?"

He leaned into her hand. She had a pleasant berry smell.

"Well, come on now. I've got lunch waiting." She took his

elbow and led him in slow, careful steps toward the house. They jingled together, but he still couldn't figure out the source.

"There's the gate now." She guided him into the side yard and paused to pat the little dog. "Privet, Mishul." The table would be twelve steps forward, then three right. Anton could find it all very well on his own, but he liked the feel of her, large and soft, against his side. "Here's our table. You take this seat right here." She placed his hand against the chair and he sat down to their usual lunch in the shade of the root shed. On the table he could smell fried potatoes and tomato salad with vinegar. Oleg got close behind him and hummed "zzzzzzzz" in his ear.

"Oleg, stop that. What is that?" she said.

"Nothing."

When she went into the house for more bread, Anton whispered, "What's the jingling?"

"Earrings," Oleg said with a mouthful. "She's trying to impress Sasha next door now that his wife's dead."

Oleg's grandmother returned. "I hear you're going to the dentist tomorrow."

Anton nodded.

"They have these long metal picks they stick right into your teeth." Oleg hammered his fork against his plate.

"Be quiet, Oleg," she said.

"It's true," he went on. "I saw it on television. They drill big holes in your teeth."

Anton put down his bread and ran his tongue along his molars.

"See what a coward Oleg is? But you're not afraid, are you, Anton?"

"No," he said, pushing his chin up, hoping his face wouldn't give him away.

Dr. Nicholson worked at a practice for the new rich and the foreigners, and it was supposed to be painless, but Anton had his doubts. It was some kind of exchange program for introducing new tactics to the Russian dentists, and his schedule was full all the time. Anton's mother had been working as the cleaning lady at his summer house for almost a year now, and he paid her in dollars, not rubles. He had an apartment in the city and a place back in America probably, and a two-story cottage in Drezna that he visited only one or two weekends a month. Anton's mother took care of the garden, which was hard in this dry summer, and she cleaned up before and after him when he visited. The pay was outrageous; she made more in one month than Anton's father, before he left them, had ever made in a year. Sometimes Dr. Nicholson paid her extra just to go there in the evenings and turn lights on and off as if someone were living there.

Anton's mother came home with fresh stories all the time. *Dr. Nicholson has a computer at his cottage. Dr. Nicholson has a new car. Dr. Nicholson is learning Russian, really talking, using the right cases and everything. Today we sat down for tea together.* She hummed songs all evening after that day.

The most remarkable thing about Dr. Nicholson was his teeth. "So white and perfect they're almost . . . unnatural. No wonder they brought him all this way. It makes me almost afraid to smile."

One night she came home and taught Anton how to smile without opening his lips, and how not to leave his mouth hanging open all the time. They sat together with their fingers on each other's mouths, practicing. "That's pretty good, Anton," she said in the end. "Before long you'll be turning heads yourself." Anton had gaps between his teeth.

By early spring his mother had saved enough for an appointment of her own. The Herbalife diet was over and she was thin and, as everyone said, lovely, and she wanted her teeth to be as good as she was. Dr. Nicholson fit her into his schedule and gave her 25 percent off. *Americans are known for their generosity.* And though she came home that night saying, "Truly it was almost painless," her voice seemed constricted, and she kept getting up in the night, popping open the aspirin bottle. But the neighbors said she had a Hollywood smile.

Now she had saved enough again to give Anton a turn. She had already told everyone they knew.

"Just wait till you meet Dr. Nicholson," she said when she put Anton to bed that night. "I think you'll really like him."

Anton lay very still.

"You'll be nice to him, won't you, druzhok?"

Anton wanted to tell her that his teeth were just fine, that they never bothered or hurt him at all. They were hard and clicked together when he chewed; there was nothing rotten or soft about them. A dentist was unnecessary. Dr. Nicholson in general could go back from where he came.

But she leaned, thin and new, over him in the bed and brushed his hair back. "Just think how handsome you'll be for all the girls."

She stroked her thumbs along his eyelids to make him sleepy. Anton could tell she was smiling. He could just feel it.

They had to start out early in the morning and with good clothes on. Anton's ironed shirt pinched at his wrists, and his pants felt tight against his thighs and groin when he walked. But by the time they'd made it halfway to the train station on the dusty, rutted road, the sun was warm on their necks, and his clothes seemed to stretch out a little with the perspiration.

"This is the big day, right?" she said.

He didn't want to talk about it.

"You'll see. It won't even hurt a bit."

He ran his tongue between his lip and his upper teeth, letting it slip in and out between the gaps. They might be gone by the end of the day. There was no telling what could happen. His breath was fresh, his teeth just brushed and slick.

"Think how handsome you'll be," she said, then stumbled and put a hand on his shoulder to steady herself in the ruts.

When they reached the train platform they stood on the cement with the morning commuters, shuffling their feet.

"Lucky we don't have to do this every day, right? We are truly lucky people."

"Do you go this way to Dr. Nicholson's cottage?"

"I go the other direction. I go southeast, which is that way." She held out his arm a little forward and to the left.

"So the city is that way?" Anton pointed his other hand in the opposite direction.

"Good. And show me south."

He pointed.

"Umnik moi. Such a smart boy." The platform started to quiver, and his mother moved in close behind him and held his shoulders with both hands to protect him. The *elektrichka* rumbled in; it was quieter but seemed to move faster than the regular trains. Soon Anton's mother was guiding him forward in the shuffle of bodies, and he was pushed up against the backs of the commuters. "Watch out," said an old woman as he stumbled on something she was carrying. Then she paused and said, "Oh, sorry."

"Here, quick." His mother tried to guide him to a seat before they filled up. The train was already thick with the breath and newspaper scent of people from towns farther out. "Oh, here we go." She patted his hand to a seat. He sat down and felt the thigh of a woman next to him on the bench. She seemed to scoot away from him. He could feel his mother still standing next to him on the aisle, shuffling forward each time someone passed by.

"No, you sit, Mama." He stood up.

"I'm fine, dear." She pressed down on his shoulder.

"Really." He stood up, spread his legs for balance, locked his knees.

"Well, all right. Here." She sat down and shifted behind him, then pulled him down by the hips to sit on her lap the way children do. He lost his balance and landed on her, sitting there for a moment as she wished. But she had grown smaller, or he had gotten bigger. He felt ridiculous, too big, and he pushed away from her, standing back up.

"No."

And so they stayed like this, she on the seat, he clutching the seat back with one hand and her shoulder with the other, swaying with the motion of the train for over an hour in the morning odors of the passengers. Aftershave, alcohol, cigarettes, coffee. The freshness of his own breath started to make him feel separate at first, and then a little nauseated, and his mouth began to water. They passed the stops for Nazarevo, Kazanskoe, and Esino, and the humming and screeching of the train accelerating and braking each time filled his thoughts with drills and strange metal pokers and instruments. He started to sweat at the brow and under his arms.

He closed his eyes and tried to breathe deeply for a while, thinking of Oleg's picture girls and the stream and the sun and the tomatoes and dust that would be there when he returned. He touched the folded bills in his pocket. There were nine of them. It would be nice to be able to help Oleg for a change. It would be nice to be the one who held the treasure.

The closer they got to the city the more crowded the train became, until finally he didn't have to hold on to his mother's shoulder because it was too crowded for him to fall down. When the doors opened at Kurskii Vokzal in Moscow the warm, damp bodies in the aisle pushed forward with such force that Anton's mother lost her grip on him, bruising his wrist in one last attempt to snatch him, and she had to call after the babushka next to him, "Help my boy off. He's blind. Hold my boy." Anton cringed, and the woman grabbed his arm so that her bag banged hard against his thigh. When they reached the steps the woman called out, "Hold still for a minute, thugs, we've got a blind boy here."

"There's the step. There you go. There's another one, little guy." She held tightly to his arm on the platform until his mother arrived. "Thank you."

Anton blinked his eyes against the insult of this woman's hand on his arm. But the air of the open station yard felt cool on his skin and contained a hundred unfamiliar smells.

"This city," his mother said. "I don't see how people can stand it. Let's go."

They walked arm in arm up the platform toward the noise of the station buildings. Women in heels clicked erratically around them, people brushed past them and overcame them from behind, and all the while the trains were coming and going with the *ding dong dong* of the departure announcements.

"Where to now?"

"We'll go down to the metro station and take it through the center, then transfer down to Profsoyuznaya," she said.

"Is it far?"

"We have plenty of time. Hold still. Let me wipe your face."

"What direction are we going now?"

"This is"—she stopped walking a moment and turned around a little—"I think this is south."

"That's south," a man next to them said.

"Oh. We're going east right now, dear."

They walked on toward the station buildings, and the sound from the loudspeakers got louder. There was the smell of shashlik grills already being fired up to the right where the cafés and kiosks must be. Some men brushed past them smelling of fish and stale alcohol. They were speaking a strange, jumbled language.

Anton inhaled and gathered his courage, then squeezed his mother's arm. "I'd like to buy a magazine," he said.

"What?"

"For Oleg. Oleg wants a certain . . . he wants a car magazine."

"A car magazine? What for?"

"I don't know. He likes them."

"Car magazines. What will it be next?" She stopped and pulled him out of the line of traffic. He could feel her body leaning in different directions, looking for the right kiosk. Then she led him a few steps to their right, which Anton figured must be south. They were up against the cool metal of a kiosk now; it was still damp from the morning. A man leaned in over Anton's shoulder and said, "*Komsomolets*," then shifted to reach for his paper. Anton's mother pulled him to the side again.

"What kind of car magazine?"

"Do they have a lot of magazines? Is it a well-stocked kiosk?"

"They're all well stocked nowadays. What they wouldn't sell you. Which one do you want? They have *Avtomobil* from May and July, and two foreign ones—that one has a lovely purple car. Very strange."

Anton paused.

"Well? What do you think he'd like?"

"I think . . . I think he has those already. I think it's supposed to have a truck. Something with a truck."

His mother asked the woman through the window about trucks. They didn't have any truck magazines.

"But they have lots of magazines?"

"Yes. Do you want a different one?"

He could be grown-up like Oleg. They could be equal.

"Do you have to go to the bathroom, Mama?"

"Anton, stop this. What is this about?"

"I . . . I—" A mechanical female voice interrupted him through the speakers over his head, announcing the departure of the next train to Kursk. Anton felt as though he were being swallowed up by her voice, by the vibrating speakers everywhere, by the crush of strangers poking in at him through the void before his eyes. "I have to go to the bathroom," he said.

"You have to go to the bathroom." Her words came out slowly, but Anton could hear the frustration welling in them. She pulled him toward her by both shoulders and snapped her words into his face. "Anton. This isn't funny."

He'd had enough too. "I know."

"Well, you'll have to wait till Dr. Nicholson's. We're not going in any train station bathroom. I'll tell you that for sure."

"I'm going to be sick," he lied. He didn't know what he was doing. In his mind a vague plan was struggling to take shape. His muscles stiffened one by one and a cold tingle swept up his limbs to his throat. He clenched his jaw against the idea of Dr. Nicholson's instruments and imagined himself taller and broad shouldered, strong. He imagined himself so big that his mother couldn't drag him anywhere. "I'm going to be sick," he said again.

She sighed. She lightened her grip on his arm. They started walking again, eastward. One, two, three, four, five, six, seven, eight. She paused and asked someone about a bathroom. "Inside by the ticket booths," a man said.

"Didn't you go before we left?"

Twenty-nine. Thirty. Thirty-one. "I guess not." They turned right. Forty-eight, forty-nine, through heavy doors that pushed in both directions, into a heat wave of bodies standing sweating in lines, foreign voices, more announcement bells, a puddle, and down six steps, then around a landing and down seven more. Fifty-six, fifty-seven, to the right. He could find his way back to the kiosk alone. Seventy-four, seventy-five, seventy-six. They stopped. He could take a breath in the bathroom and calm himself, break free of her and find his way back to the kiosk and to Drezna and the tomato fields and the Shurins. He could do that. She could go see Dr. Nicholson without him.

They had neared the bathrooms: The smell of waste seeped through the air. "We'll have to wait for help," his mother said. She was breathing heavy with disgust. It was an area where no one would choose to stand around.

"I can do it alone."

"No."

He shuffled and squirmed. "I'm sick, Mama. I'm sick."

"Excuse me." She reached out to a man passing by. No response. They waited. "Excuse me," she said again to another. "My son needs to go to the bathroom." No response. He must have walked away.

"I can do it myself."

"I said no."

"*Excuse me.*" This time her voice was urgent. And she must have gotten someone's attention, for it turned soft again. "My son here needs to go to the bathroom. Be kind, would you take him in for me? He's blind, see."

"Well, hello." The man smelled of yesterday's cabbage soup.

His mother drove a finger into his back. "Hello," he said.

"Well, let's go then."

His face was hot. He took the man's arm, which felt frail under his textured suit jacket.

"You can do everything yourself, right?" the man asked in a low voice as they walked through the door and deeper into the stench.

"Yes. Of course." The floor was wet and slippery.

"How did it happen, may I ask?"

"What?"

"The eyes."

Hundred seven. Eight. Nine, right on nine. The room was quiet except for a faucet dripping somewhere.

"Don't like to talk about it?"

Anton said nothing. He didn't know how it had happened. He was born to this.

"That's all right. Here you go." The man took Anton's hand and placed it against the cool porcelain of the urinal. "Don't touch it too much, but here it is right in front of you. Is that all right?"

If there were another door he could slip out of, if he could make himself small, unnoticeable, he could slip away from this old man and his cabbage smell and count his way right back to the kiosk. One hundred nine steps was nothing; it was half the distance from Oleg's house to the river. And he could ask someone for help if he got lost. He could do it. He could slap his bills down for the lady in the kiosk and say *Pentxaus* with authority, without fear or hesitation of any kind. He would walk away a man, like any normal man, with the magazine tucked into his pants under his shirt. He would catch the next train to Drezna and be back in time for lunch with Oleg and Grandma Shurin. And she'd be sorry, his mother. She would worry and worry. She would think twice about her American dentist.

"Is there another door in here?"

"What?" The man shuffled around a little and came back to Anton's side. "No. Just the one."

The dripping faucet echoed against the walls and floor around him. Anton felt his face beginning to twitch.

"Well, what's the problem, son?"

There was nowhere he could go.

"I need a toilet."

"Oh, I see. Right." He took Anton's arm again and turned him around, but in turning the old man slipped on the wet tile and began to go down. "Oi!" He clutched at Anton's torso with both arms, pressing Anton's head into his hot, damp chest. They wavered a moment, flailing, but did not go down. They stood upright on the tile floor, trembling, without so much as a bumped elbow to knock the thrill out of their bones.

All of his numbers were gone, flown from his head. All his bearings, all his points of reference. He didn't even know where the door was. He wasn't going to get to the kiosk alone, or to the train or Drezna or anywhere. He was a little boy clutching at an old man in a stinking threadbare suit in the basement reek of Kurskii Vokzal, with his mother worrying at the door. And he was not sick at all, though the stench was enough to turn anyone's stomach, and Oleg was home in the field pulling weeds and dreaming of his girls without so much as a thought for Anton or the money he'd given him.

"Well, are you going in or not?" the man said, pressing Anton's hand against the gritty door of the stall.

He stood in his tight pants with his hand on the metal door. "Go to hell," Anton murmured. From behind them came the click of dress shoes and then the sound of someone urinating.

"Pardon?"

"You heard me," Anton whispered.

"This is how you treat an old man?"

"Go to hell."

This time the man slapped him. Not on the face, like his mother did on rare occasion. On the behind. He spanked him.

The tears came now; there was no chance of stopping them. "Pervert," Anton hissed in one last attempt at manliness. "Get your hands off me."

"What's going on here?" the dress-shoes man at the urinal said.

"Kids. Kids today don't know how to behave."

"Stop touching me!" Anton cried. "Don't *touch* me." The old man removed his hand and took a step back, and now Anton was alone against the door of the stall, sinking down. He crouched low on the wet, filthy floor, and the tears came. He sucked at the air in unsteady patches. There was no one anywhere, not even the foreigners, who could fix this.

"Dorogoi moi," his mother's voice came rushing in. She crouched down on the floor and folded him in her arms.

"What have you done?" she hissed at the old man.

"He's crazy," the old man said.

"I just found them like this," said the man who had been at the urinal.

And then the room seemed to clear out and get quiet, and she rocked him there on the floor against her chest, back and forth. She let him erupt in her arms without asking questions. She stroked his hair and the back of his neck and said, "That's all right, druzhok. That's all right."

"I don't want to go to Dr. Nicholson's."

"You're sick. It's all right." She stroked his back. "You're not feeling well."

In time it subsided and Anton was left feeling hollow, his nose wet, his voice deep and thick with mucous.

"Let's get out of here," she said. "How about that?"

"Let's go, let's go. I want to go home."

So they wiped themselves off and she straightened his clothes. They stood very upright and walked together out of the men's room in the basement of the station, and whether anybody was watching them he did not know, but he knew that his mother had been a great beauty in her day and that she carried herself very nicely, always in top form, and she was thin now and supple at his side, and he was proud to be with her. They walked an even forty steps straight ahead this way, as if on parade with their shoulders back, breathing deeply, and then they went up the seven stairs and around the landing, up six more, and through the swinging doors out of the stink and heat toward the left into the open cement yard of the station. The loud speakers were at it still but the morning rush had subsided, and they were able to walk freely without being jostled. It was twenty-nine steps to the ice cream stand with the heat of the sun on their faces, and at the window she gave Anton the money and let him order for them, two Eskimos. They walked back to their platform holding the ice cream bars, cold in their hands, not opening the wrappers until they had reached a bench in the middle of the platform where they could feel the push and pull of the trains coming in and going out as they waited for the next one leaving toward Drezna.

SPECTATORS

THEY DROVE THE eighty miles from Elgin up to Delavan Lake on cruise control without saying more than a few tight, courteous words. Marion had been experimenting with reticence lately. Though she had told Arnie not to take it personally, he found it hard not to add this to his list of worries. When they parked at the golf course he wanted to help her out of the car and stand next to her as she took her first look at the place, the event, but she flapped her hand at him and made the face that said he was starting to act old again. She pushed her door open wide and scooted herself around sideways, lifting her left leg with one hand and setting it down outside on the pavement. From inside the car he watched her hoist herself upright onto her good leg and then straighten her pants out where they tended to catch in the socket of her prosthesis, though they hadn't caught this time. She didn't get her cane out of the back seat. One of the things she liked about the golfing, he suspected, was that she could use her driver for support instead. And she was getting better with the walking. She could go eight or ten steps on a flat surface without a cane or a golf club or anything. All in all she was doing really well, Arnie thought. That was what he told everyone. There was nothing to be afraid of; she'd be fine.

But when he got out of the car he could see the shadow of a grimace on her. "Nothing," she said when he asked her about it. It was a bright blue day, already hot before eight in the morning, and the golf course stretched out calmly around them, as if waiting. Marion wasn't looking at the soft curves and dales of the ninth fairway though; she was squinting with distaste at the big orange plastic banner overhead, which made a rough clapping sound each time the breeze shifted. SIXTH ANNUAL MIDWEST REGIONAL AMPUTEE GOLF TOURNAMENT it said in black letters.

"Subtle," she muttered.

She avoided the vocabulary of this new predicament, threw away the booklets from her prosthetist and physical therapists, stashed the ointments, kept the leg itself perpetually hidden under pants.

"Sixth annual. They must be doing something right," Arnie tried, but she wouldn't meet his gaze. "Let's get someone from inside to help with your clubs."

"Oh. Can't you do it, Arn?" she said absently.

He hesitated. "Sure. Sure." He bent over the open trunk and braced himself for the needles that would punch into his back and legs, starting with the two herniated discs between his shoulder blades and moving down past his knees.

Suddenly Marion gasped. Poking his head out of the trunk, Arnie saw it too: pairs of suntanned players, smiling, chatting, moving with their mismatched limbs and herky-jerky gaits from the clubhouse to the neat rows of golf carts waiting in the shade. "Oh God." Marion turned away from them. "Here they come."

Arnie himself had never been any good at golf, though he had always appreciated the tidy green isolation of golf courses, the way people's voices dropped naturally to church tones, as if there were something in their midst to worship. He liked the cocktails and groundskeepers and the old-fashioned shoes, and the way serious adults could abandon the jagged concerns of their lives to focus for a few quiet hours on the flight of a small dimpled ball. There was a kind of frivolous beauty in that, a weightlessness.

When they were first married, back in the sixties, Arnie had often caught men watching Marion as she teed off. In the brief seconds following her swing, while she stood, mouth ajar, eyes tracing the ball's quick sweep over the fairway, Arnie liked to glance back to watch the people watching her. From the clubhouse lawn or adjacent holes, they shook their heads, eyebrows raised. Sometimes a faint whistle escaped through their teeth; he could hear it.

Now he stood on the cart path behind the first tee, watching as Marion bent low to the ground to tee up her ball and then wobbled herself upright again. She'd spent weeks getting this move right in physical therapy, and each time he watched her do it, Arnie felt himself clench up and concentrate, praying she wouldn't fall. If she glanced back at him now, he would give her a quick thumbs up. But she didn't. She just took two quick practice swings, then squared up to the ball, inhaled, and hit it. Nowadays, she really only took half a swing, all from the shoulders and restrained, as if she feared she could knock herself off her feet if she really let loose. But still, he liked to watch her. Each skill she reacquired seemed like a brick rebuilding her. When her ball cleared the water hazard and landed just a few feet off the fairway, in the fringe but not the rough, he couldn't help clapping and saying, "There you go, girl."

The other golfers in her foursome made encouraging noises, but Marion just shook her head and walked back to Arnie.

"It's a good start," he said. "Really."

"So you'll wait here at the clubhouse?" she asked. Most of the other spouses and friends had already cleared out, looking for other things to do at the resort.

"I'll sit right there on the patio."

"In case I get tired or something," she said. This had been one of her conditions before agreeing to come: If she wanted to quit early, back out, he'd be right there to take her home. No questions, no guilt trips.

"I remember. I promise."

"OK, then," Marion said, moving away as he reached for her. "Off you go."

He walked back to the clubhouse patio to join the few remaining spectators, leaving her alone then, shyly withdrawn from her foursome. The organizers had put her with two men from Indiana who appeared to be friends, and a woman from Black Earth whose left leg stopped just below the hip. She wore no prosthesis, and Arnie watched as she dropped her crutches near the edge of the tee and hopped into place. After only one practice swing, she steadied herself again and smacked the ball low and straight, almost a hundred yards.

"Wow," Arnie said before thinking, unable to suppress his surprise.

"Yeah, she's something, huh?" said a voice behind him.

It was a red-haired woman about his age sitting and smoking at one of the tables on the patio. The man sitting next to her had removed his C-Leg and was poking at the knee joint with an allen wrench.

"You'd think she'd want a prosthesis at least just for balance," Arnie said.

"Too high up," the woman said, touching the side of her hand to the top of her thigh. "You have to have something to fit it on."

Arnie's face reddened. "Of course."

"Shoot, sometimes I think I'd be better off without this one," the man next to her said, tapping his leg on the table.

It was nice of him to try to put others at ease like that. They introduced themselves—Bill and Cheryl Tider, from Arlington Heights—and gestured for Arnie to join them. He sat down at their table, all the while keeping his eye on Marion as her group got into their carts and jerked into motion, speeding over the little bridge and down toward the fairway. It felt like the morning, decades ago, when he first brought their daughter Elizabeth to her new school in Elgin after he'd been transferred. "Give 'em hell," he had said, patting her shoulder to nudge her toward the other kids on the playground. She'd refused to say good-bye or turn back and wave, though he stood there for twenty minutes, even after she'd gone in the building.

"So, she just gets around with those crutches like that?" Arnie asked this couple, shifting his thoughts back to Marion's golf partner.

Cheryl gave a big nod. "Lost her leg as a little girl, some kind of farming accident. She told me once, but I can't remember the specifics. Anyway, big farm family like that, she had to just get around however she could. They've got three kids, too."

"Hooh." Arnie shook his head.

"I always find it inspiring here," Cheryl said.

"Where's your inspiration when I'm searching for the remote control?" Bill said.

"You poor baby."

Arnie watched them closely. "Can I help with the leg?" he asked. Until last year he'd been a mechanical engineer all his life, designing and reconfiguring parts for generators. After the accident it seemed best to retire a couple years early, but he missed the job sometimes, the figuring and drafting, the public demands on his time.

"I'm not getting the right swivel action in the knee joint," Bill said, glancing around at the last few groups of golfers, who were about to leave without him.

"It's because you've gained weight again," Cheryl said. "It always breaks down when you get heavy."

"Ah!" Bill cried, snapping his hand back. "That's it. I got it." He picked up the leg and showed Arnie the swivel action of the knee.

"There you go," Arnie said, feeling useless again.

Bill pushed his shorts up to his hip and fitted the leg back onto his stump, pulling the Velcro strip through the hole at the bottom of the socket and securing it into place on top of his thigh. He stood up and took a few tentative steps and turns.

"That'll have to do." He kissed Cheryl on the forehead and shook Arnie's hand, then went off to join the others. Most of them were men who, like Bill, wore their artificial arms and legs without the flesh-colored covering that was meant to help them blend in. In their shorts and polo shirts, they let their plastic and metal parts glint freely in the sun.

"Did the women go out in earlier rounds?" Arnie asked. Aside from the woman Marion was playing with, Arnie had only seen two or three ladies among the dozens of players.

Cheryl shook her head. "There just aren't very many ladies at these things for some reason. Never have been."

"Huh," Arnie said. He'd hoped Marion would make friends, lady friends, with people who had gone through this and come out the other side. It seemed to Arnie that she was still in the middle, alone, drifting further from him all the time.

While the patio emptied out Cheryl chatted with a few other wives that she knew, and two of them sat down at the table and joined them. Arnie relaxed into their small talk, letting his eyes settle over the manicured stretches of fairway reaching out around them. Marion's group had gone out of sight behind the trees, but if he understood the map correctly, they would come back into view in another few holes, far off in the distance where he could make out the sixth tee. The golf course was old and elegantly designed, with impressive oak trees and water hazards and artfully carved out sand traps. The perennial gardens near the tees and greens were overflowing with blooms, and the cart paths were solid tar black, recently repaved. He was concerned about Marion, but he had to admit it was pleasant, sitting here, making conversation in the morning sun with such cheerful women. He'd been living on tiptoes, keeping quiet, for so many months.

The others at the table had been coming to these tournaments for years and knew all the stories about the different players. Cheryl and Bill had even gone to the national tournament twice, in Arizona.

"He's not terribly competitive though," Cheryl said, giving Arnie and the other women a look.

"Well." Arnie understood her meaning. "All my life I never once beat Marion in a golf game. Until now." The mood was light, and he had smiled when saying this, but once it was out of his mouth the comment felt sour. "It's awkward," he said, after a moment.

"Oh, and who cares about scores," another woman said. "Such a stupid game, paying all this money to get angry at a little ball."

Everyone laughed, and Arnie relaxed again.

"Well, I don't know about you all," Cheryl said, "but I was toying with the idea of embarking on a cocktail."

The sun had risen in the sky, it was after eleven, and they were all leaning close to the table to catch the shade of the umbrella.

"It *is* sort of a holiday," one woman said.

"Count me in." Arnie smiled. They got a deck of cards from

the bartender and passed the time playing gin rummy and drinking Bloody Marys. For a long time Arnie kept his gaze on that sixth tee, looking for Marion in her pale yellow outfit and visor. He liked to imagine she was making friends too, or at least shooting well. With so few women in the tournament, he realized, she was practically guaranteed to win a trophy.

"So your wife just recently lost her leg?" one of Cheryl's friends was asking him.

Arnie nodded. "Not quite a year ago."

Cheryl shook her head. "How did it happen?"

"Car accident," Arnie said. The women held his gaze, waiting for something more, the full story, because by now Arnie had been filled in on the sad, terrible stories of all their husbands and several of the other golfers as well—people he hadn't even met. He inhaled and stared back at them, tempted. He had heard Marion brush off this question so many times that he always automatically followed her lead: *Dumb luck, just a car accident. It could happen to anyone.* For the most part, this was the truth anyway, or as much of the truth as mattered.

But in the bright sun like this, after those cocktails, staring at these kind women, Arnie felt maybe he could say something more about what he had seen that day in the car with Marion. Something, maybe, about how it had felt being pinched in next to his wife in that small, crushed space, feeling the strange new jabs of pain in his back while they waited for what seemed like hours for the sirens to come. Marion had drifted in and out. When she was conscious, terrible moans and wheezing came from her mouth, and her eyes blazed into him with raw animal shock. In the moments she went under and got peaceful again Arnie couldn't help himself: He shook her arm and yelled at her to come back, come back right this minute. In a revolting trick of memory, the smell of those awful moments returned to him—blood, tires, urine. But just then he saw her, Marion, not small and far away on the sixth tee but driving right up to the clubhouse in that golf cart, glaring at him. It was unsettling to see her behind the wheel, for she rarely drove anything anymore. She was alone, without her partner, without her group, and her face was stricken. He closed his mouth. He got up and went to her.

"Well, that was fun," Marion said, her eyes dark, steely globes. Her face was pinched up and damp.

"What happened, honey?"

"Nothing," she said. "Can we please just get going?"

"Sure." Arnie squatted to hoist her golf bag off the cart and shouldered it up. He waved to the others and followed Marion slowly back to the parking lot.

"You don't have to walk behind me like that," she said. "It's like you're constantly waiting to catch me in some horrible collapse. It makes me nervous."

Arnie set his jaw and counted to five. He let her open her own car door. He wrestled the clubs into the trunk and got in on the driver's side. It was less than a quarter mile on the empty resort road from the clubhouse to the hotel over by the lake's edge, but he took the route slowly, thinking of the cocktails. "Is the leg bothering you, Marion?" From the others today he had learned that the type of suction socket she used gave a lot of people trouble, especially on hot days—blisters, heat rash, chafing. But Marion had never mentioned any of these problems.

"Arnie, you asked me to try this tournament and I tried it. Can we please just go home now?"

"Sure," he said, pretending she had said hotel instead of home. "We'll just go check in and you can take a nap if you want before the banquet."

Marion shivered and turned from him, but she didn't put up a fight. Arnie could feel her removing herself from her body, from the car, drifting out the window and away from him so that none of this could touch her.

"Marion," he said quietly, to bring her back.

She didn't move.

In the hotel room Arnie unpacked their things and drew her a bath. He unfolded the walker she used whenever her leg was off, and put it next to the armchair where she was sitting. At home, lately Marion had been dressing and undressing in private, but here there was just the one big room and the bathroom. Arnie wondered if he ought to excuse himself, go downstairs awhile to give her some space, but he was tired, and tired of giving her that. Exactly when things had come to be this way was unclear to him; in the early weeks after they got out of the hospital, she had let Arnie help her with everything—bathing, the bathroom, dressing. She had let him see her in every imaginable state. And he didn't mind it. He was good at it. This was his wife, alive and conscious; they had survived. But over time, once she started walking with crutches and then the new leg, Arnie felt her pulling away from him, hiding everything, using each new bit of independence against him.

From her chair she looked at her leg, then at him, then gave a sigh and went into the bathroom fully clothed, taking the walker with her.

"Would you like me to help you?" he said, but she closed the door.

Arnie lay back on the bed and tried not to think so much. He took his pain pills and did his back stretches, then found his phone and dialed their daughter out east.

"Well, I just wanted to give you the number here," he said. It was a silly excuse—she didn't need a hotel number when he had his cell—but Elizabeth let it go.

"Your mother's just resting after the first round." Arnie stared up at the dusty globs of spackle on the textured ceiling. He tried to picture Elizabeth's new condo outside Boston, which he hadn't yet seen. "She did real well. I imagine she'll probably get a trophy."

"Really."

"Well, there aren't that many women," he admitted.

"Dad," she said, searching for words. "Just don't . . . I mean, do you have to—?"

"She loves the golf, honey." Arnie tried to make his voice bright. "You should see her. She's still better than half the women at our club." There was no way to tell Elizabeth about the days and days Marion had spent curled up on their bed with pillows over her face, refusing to brush her teeth or wash, refusing to speak. If Elizabeth wanted to think he was pushing Marion too hard, he could live with that.

"Sure. But a tournament's a whole different thing from a quiet game at home."

"You should see the people here, Lizzie. How well they handle it."

"Like how?" she said.

"I don't know. Just, they do. Very pleasant people."

Elizabeth waited for him to elaborate.

Triumphant was the word that came to him, though it seemed ridiculous to say such a word aloud.

"Well, that's good, Dad," Elizabeth said politely. "I'm glad it's good for you. Can I talk to Mom?"

This was the way most of their phone conversations ended. Arnie tapped lightly on the bathroom door, then opened it a crack and spoke without looking in.

"Honey, Lizzie's on the phone. Do you want to talk to her?"

"Hang on," Marion said. "OK."

When he opened the door the beige shower curtain had been pulled across the tub so that only Marion's arm stuck out, disembodied, reaching for the telephone. He put it in her palm and left again.

In the other room Arnie sat in the armchair against the bathroom wall and listened. The words were muffled and bleary, but the rise and fall of her voice was unmistakably lively, the way it used to be, with Arnie and with everyone. There was no reticence. After a while he even heard the traces of laughter. It occurred to him that maybe Marion was only putting on an act for Elizabeth. But again, the laughter rose up, and he heard Marion cry, "Exactly!" before the words drifted back into mush. If it was an act, it was a pretty good act.

Outside, the sky was putting on its evening colors over the lake, and Arnie sat staring out at the water, trying to remember better times. There were lots of them, decades and decades of them. They had been very fortunate, as a family, but now, when he tried to reconstruct a scene, say, from one of their old camping trips or holidays, it would crumble and drift away from him before he even got through the first moments. He concentrated on their vacation in Alaska two years ago, when Marion surprised him with a daylong boat trip, though she always got seasick, because she knew how much he wanted to see the whales. He could picture her there, rocking at the back of the boat, trying to put on a smile though her skin was downright greenish. She kept pointing out at the whales and telling him to take pictures so that he would look away from her when she needed to be sick. He could get that far into the memory, usually: the blue-black lumps of flesh breaking the surface, their white scars like chalk marks in a foreign language. Then a crash of the tail and the water hid them again. He held her hand. And now, focusing everything he had, he could also remember the two of them curled up on the hotel bed that night, eating mashed potatoes they'd ordered from room service to settle her stomach. But from there the scene quickly faded and escaped him. He knew in his brain what they had done next and next, but he could no longer see it or feel it. It was gone.

After a while the bathroom grew quiet. Arnie decided to get dressed for the banquet, so he'd be ready when Marion got out. But a long time passed and she didn't come out. There were no sounds of movement or water for over an hour.

He knocked on the bathroom door. "Marion, honey?"

She didn't answer.

He believed in her right to privacy. He did. This was not a thing you took from a woman. But he also had a sudden piercing vision of her, passed out asleep in the tub, under the water. Her naps were so deep and demanding these days that she could fall asleep sitting upright in broad daylight; he could only imagine the effect a warm bath after a hard day might have on her. He called her name again, then opened the door.

The shower curtain was drawn halfway across the tub, and Marion was dead asleep, though her face, crooked against her shoulder, was several inches from the water. "Marion," he said, blinking the lights. "Wake up."

She opened her eyes and stared at the water for a long time, opening and closing her mouth. When she finally turned her face to him she gasped. She shifted in the water, trying to cover herself, then remembered the shower curtain and pulled it closed again.

Arnie sat down on the toilet seat next to the bathtub. "Marion, I have seen you naked for forty-odd years."

"Please, Arnie."

He sat quietly, elbows on knees, chin on hands, waiting for some kind of words to come to him.

"It has been my privilege," he said.

"Oh, for God's sake," Marion said, but with a lilt of laughter in her voice.

"I remember that time in the Wisconsin Dells," he said, "when you did that little striptease in our motel room." Marion grunted behind the curtain, but Arnie went on thinking about it. This was when Elizabeth was about six months old, once Marion was starting to feel like her own person again, and Arnie's mother had agreed to watch the baby while they went away for their anniversary weekend.

"I remember thinking how strange it was. Don't get me wrong, it was sweet. That you still thought any of it mattered, the physical stuff. The visuals."

They were quiet for a moment, then Marion said, "I'm not going to that banquet tonight."

"Who's talking about the banquet?"

"You're trying to butter me up, and I'm just saying, it's not going to work."

Behind the curtain the water sloshed around, and Marion turned on the faucet to add more hot water.

"Marion, if you gave these people a chance."

"I gave them a chance. And to tell you the truth"—she searched for the right words—"they disgusted me."

"Marion—"

"I spent the whole blessed morning watching them show off their fake parts. I must have heard the words *bionic man* five times. As if they're proud of it."

"Maybe they *are* proud of it."

"Give me a break. And then"—she got more excited, even

pulling back the curtain a few inches to make eye contact with him—"they started telling these horrible stories," she said. "You couldn't even say 'pleased to meet you' without having to hear all about their miserable tragedies."

"I got that too." Arnie smiled. They were talking. "Yeah. It's interesting."

"The worst moment of their lives, and they want to peddle it around to perfect strangers."

"Maybe it's just part of the whole process of getting used to this new life. In a year or two, maybe you'll think it's the most ordinary thing."

"Why on earth"—she turned on him, suddenly glaring—"would I ever want to do that?"

Arnie sat silently, wishing he knew that magic trick she'd learned in the accident, the ability to slip away, evaporate from your most unbearable moments. He envied her.

"Why don't you just go," she said, "to the banquet down there, without me. If you like these people so much."

"I will," he said, first bluffing, then meaning it. "I will. As soon as you get out of that tub."

"Arnie—"

"You're going to pass out in there. I can see it." His voice rose up beyond his control. "And I'll come back later and find you dead under the water."

The words echoed over the tile like a wish.

"Get out," she said.

Arnie stood up, swelling, wanting to be elsewhere, unconnected, but here he was, dumb socks stuck on the wet tile, dumb white hairs poking out of him everywhere in the mirror. On his way out he punched furiously at the curtain, which gave way only briefly before falling back into place.

Downstairs, the banquet room was empty. An hour early, Arnie paced by the doorway, alone with his useless anger. On the table next to him someone had arranged dozens of name tags in perfect little rows, with so many pairs of matching surnames. Arnie couldn't stand them. He scooped one hand across a row, but the pins snagged on the tablecloth and only five or six took flight. Then suddenly a group of little boys in swimsuits raced through the hallway screaming, leaving their wet footprints and echoes everywhere. Arnie stepped out to scold them, to tell them to slow down, but they disappeared around a corner, their little brains already deleting him from their day.

He went back in the room, kneeled down, and picked up the name tags. Rearranged them. Pinned his own name on. Marion's he left there with the others.

He walked down the winding hall past an arcade room and a coffee shop, until finally he came to a dark, wood-paneled room that had a long bar at one end. There were wide bay windows behind the bar, so that you could look out on the lake as you drank. The only other person at the bar was a young man sitting alone with a beer. Arnie took a seat one space away from him and ordered a beer himself.

"Are you here for the golf tournament?" Arnie said after a while.

The young man turned and nodded, and Arnie saw that he

was scarcely more than a teenager, maybe not even old enough to drink.

"Is it your parents who are playing? Or your, uh, wife?"

"No. *I'm* playing." The boy smiled and lifted his other hand up from where it had been hidden under the bar. When he waved it around Arnie could see it was really only half a hand: He had his thumb and forefinger, but the rest of his palm and all the other fingers were gone.

"Oh, I'm sorry," Arnie said, trying to act casual. "Well, how'd you shoot today?"

The boy shrugged. "Pretty good. I got a seventy-eight."

"Holy cow," Arnie said. "You going to win the whole tournament?"

"We'll see," the boy said. "How about you? You here with your wife or something?"

"Yeah, my wife's playing. She's an above-the-knee. I don't think she did too well today though."

"It's a tough course," the kid said. They sat quietly for a long time, watching the water-skiers out on the lake. There was a ramp set up in the bay, and some kids were trying to do tricks jumping off it, but mostly they kept falling on the landings, sending up great splashes of thick, greenish water.

"I was surprised there weren't more women players," Arnie said after a while.

"Oh, you know why that is, don't you?" The kid smiled.

Arnie waited.

"Women don't do nearly as much stupid risky shit as guys do." The kid laughed at this, then sobered up and said, "Seriously."

Arnie's stomach turned over. It wasn't as if everyone was here because of an accident. Sometimes it was medical—cancer or blood clots or diabetes—and sometimes people were just born this way. "Well, how did yours happen?" Arnie asked.

"Ah, stupidest thing ever. I've got 'em all beat I bet."

"What happened?"

"Fireworks, you know, a cherry bomb, M-80, whatever you call it. I found it in my dad's truck and lit the fuse, then I just sort of panicked and didn't let go of it. Now that's pretty stupid." He put his hand back under the bar, between his legs.

"You must have been a little kid," Arnie said.

The boy nodded. "It was a long time ago. Hopefully I'm smarter now."

A new bartender came on shift, and when she walked over to get their next order she didn't believe the boy was of age.

"I can vouch for him," Arnie said, when the kid couldn't produce a driver's license. "Born in 1988, October tenth. My wife was in labor with him for forty-one hours."

"Really," the bartender said. "What sign would that make him?"

"Libra," Arnie said. The bartender decided to concede defeat. It was a resort, after all; they were supposed to make people happy.

"Thanks," the kid said once she'd left. "I'm not that far off, you know."

Arnie nodded. "I heard of a guy today who lost his foot trying to jump his motorcycle over a pickup truck."

"I met that guy," the kid said. "I played a round with him last year. He's got one of those weird tall putters."

"You'd have to admit," Arnie said. "That makes a firecracker not seem so bad."

"Stupidity-wise?"

"Right."

"I suppose," the kid said. "But still." There was another long silence, when Arnie could hear the boy's teeth crunching down on the bar peanuts, and, in the background, the computerized songs of video games. Finally the boy stopped chewing and said, "So what happened to your wife?"

"Car accident," Arnie said.

"That's rough. You driving, or her?"

"Does it make a difference?" Arnie said. But of course it did.

The kid looked away, played with the label on his beer for a while. "What happened?"

It was time to follow the usual drill. Arnie shrugged. "Just, you know. Dark night, wet road. Somebody crossed over from the other side, straight at us, and before we knew it we were flipped over in the ditch. I jerked the wheel."

The boy stared at him for what felt like a long time. He had eyes like a horse, weary and huge. "Were they drunk or something?"

"No." A pocket of air escaped from Arnie's lungs, burst up through his mouth. How he'd wished for that. "No. But they died." He caught his hands making a quick jerking motion, and put them down. "It could happen to anyone, any night."

A few seconds, a few degrees in an angle, a different brand of tires. A moment of distraction, a flash of panic could cost you this much in life.

Finally the kid looked away, turned back to the window. "That's terrible."

"Stupidity-wise, it's up there," Arnie said.

Sometimes in the middle of the night Arnie would wake up to find Marion twisted away from him and shuddering, her fingers wrapped tight around the iron bars of their headboard. There were no words for this. When he tried to touch her back, she reeled away. He just had to watch.

"There's something I've always wanted to know," Arnie said. "Do you mind if I ask?"

The kid stared at him, unwilling to make any promises. Kids could be cruel. Probably this boy had heard more than his fair share of vulgar questions. But Arnie went on anyway.

"Does it ever hurt there, in the hand, you know?"

"You mean like, what do they call it, phantom pain? Nah."

"Really?"

"Nope. Not at all. I mean, maybe some people have that." He shrugged. "Not me."

"Do you ever have dreams about it, the accident?"

"I don't think so, no." He reflected for a minute. "Because in my dreams, it's still there, all whole." As he said this he spread out his bad hand next to his good one and studied them. "My mom said I slept almost constantly the whole year after it happened." The kid smiled, as if this were another of his foolish acts. "Must've been trying to dream it back or something." He laughed.

At last one of the water-skiers, a girl in a yellow life jacket with long dark hair that whipped through the air, went off the jump and landed without falling. She threw one fist up and shrieked, and the kids in the boat ahead of her applauded.

"It's probably time for the dinner by now," Arnie said. "Do you want to go?"

The kid swigged the last of his beer and tightened his jaw. "I've never really liked the banquet part. I mean, the golf is golf. The banquet is . . . No offense. It's a lot of old people."

Arnie smiled. "Of course."

"You know what I was thinking?"

"What?"

The boy squinted through the window into the setting sun and pointed at the girl waterskiing. "I was thinking I'd go introduce myself."

"Really?" Arnie said.

"Nah." The kid threw down his good hand in a dismissive gesture. The girl leaned back against the rope to spray an arc of water through the air near the pier, then dropped the rope and sunk slowly into the lake.

When he got back to the banquet the room was already full, the round tables crowded with so many happily chatting couples that Arnie felt he'd been dropped down into a wedding. He stood in the doorway kneading his back with one hand, scanning the room to see if by chance Marion had changed her mind. Cheryl and Bill waved him over to their table, which sent a pulse of relief through him, until he got closer and saw that their table was full.

"Where's your wife?" Cheryl said, working her tongue against her molars. "What's her name again?"

"Oh," Arnie said. Behind him someone whooped with laughter, startling him into a blank state. "Oh . . . we're over in the back." He pointed vaguely at a corner.

Cheryl craned her neck. "I don't see her."

"Bathroom," Arnie said. "I better get back to her." He shook Bill's hand and tried to hurry away but the room was too crowded, the aisles cluttered with canes and crutches, clogged with hobbled people. He wanted out. He was sick of them all, with their stupid afflictions. The beers were working on him. He doubled back, rerouted, waited behind an awful woman with a walker. Finally he made it to the side doors and shoved through, sucking at the air in the hallway like the room had been contaminated.

He started the long walk to their room, down the halls that were wide and muted and spooky. He tried to calm his hands, his shoulders. He mouthed out some words he could say to Marion, trying to memorize them. He always lost track. It was impossible to be angry with her, and impossible to go on.

When he reached their room an empty tray with used-up dishes was sitting in the hall. He picked up the metal cover to see what she had eaten. He was hungry, even to the point of swaying a little. When he found the remains of her cheeseburger under the cover he looked up and down the hallway and decided to eat it.

Inside, the room was already dark and quiet. He didn't care. He turned on the lights.

Marion was curled up on the bed by the window, and she didn't stir. She had turned down the blankets of the other bed as if to suggest that Arnie sleep over there. Well, he wouldn't. He went around turning on all the lights, even the TV and the radio, then he stood over her for a long time, trying to maintain his focus until she woke up. But her chest just kept rising and falling peacefully. Finally he took off his shoes, his shirt and pants. Stripped down to his underwear, he put his hand on the sheets by her neck, started pulling them back.

It was a long lavender nightgown she was wearing, one that Lizzie had given her. It was soft. To make her cold he pulled the sheets and blankets down all the way past her foot, so it was just Marion there on the blank white sheets, all alone. Still she didn't stir. Arnie took the bottom of the nightgown in his hand and pulled it up little by little, and when he got it to her thighs, he began to see. The stump was raw and chafed. There were red bumps and blisters all over, and a terrible inch-wide line rubbed raw just under her bottom, where the top of the fiberglass socket had rested all the hot day under her hip bone for support. He sucked his breath in. He turned the TV off.

Arnie went into the bathroom and washed his hands. He stared at himself in the mirror for a long time. Then he began rooting through her bag of toiletries. When he found the tube of ointment he read the pharmacist's directions to be sure, and brought it back out into the other room. On his fingers it felt cool and sticky and man-made. He touched it to her thigh as delicately as he could, fearing the skin would peel away under the slightest pressure. He dabbed and rubbed, as softly as possible, moving his eyes from her thigh up to her face every few seconds, to see whether she was still sleeping up there, still walking around in her dream world without the need of him or any canes or props. Just her. But on his next glance up he saw her eyes beginning to flicker, and he pulled back, torn between two wishes. He lifted his hand, suspending it, knowing that soon he'd be caught, there'd be questions, but first there were only her eyes, opening green, dimly searching, until they found him there in the half light and settled on him, watching, as yet uncomprehending, sweeping him up and taking him back with her.

SCAVENGERS

SO MANY PEOPLE had moved out of the neighborhood that the dogs had just about taken over. Mostly they were forlorn and peaceful, but every once in a while a frenzy of barking and low-level madness would erupt in the back alley and lurch through the side yard toward the street. At the window I'd catch their silhouettes, a group of them tussling over some piece of garbage. Then they'd settle the matter and drift apart down the middle of the wide street, where hardly any cars went anymore.

The day the girl showed up it was the odd sound of a big old car grumbling to a stop out front that drew me to the window. A dark and rusting Cadillac stood there, its back corner hanging so low I expected a huge fat man to emerge, but when the door popped and swung open it was just a scrawny girl in black jeans and several layers of sweatshirts. She had dark, bobbed hair that clung to her head damply. A little older than me, midtwenties maybe.

When she rang my doorbell I watched her for a while from the window, trying to decide if she had the jittery anxious look of a dangerous person. I'd already heard every kind of endless tall tale from the desperate types who get stranded here. They've got broken-down cars, they've been mugged or beaten, they're lost, evicted, foreclosed, someone's taken their kids. They park themselves on your porch, shivering, and break down until maybe you give them a few bucks or some leftover pizza or a ride to the bus station. You could threaten to call the cops but even they know the cops won't come. As soon as you get rid of them and have time to comb over their story you discover its many impossibilities and know you've been had. It's hard to know how to feel about yourself on such days. My dad's old friend Lenny warned me, "Tommy, it's folks like those that'll get you." Like I'll head out to jump-start their car or something and their unseen partner will come in my back door and rob me.

I don't have much to steal, I told Lenny. And his face twisted up and went sour, because he was thinking of all my dad's old things in here.

I'm making the neighborhood sound like a dirtbag haven, but it isn't. It's no Brush Park; it's not leaking mansions filled with squatters. Until the last couple of years it was pretty much normal like anyplace, rows of little two-bedroom brick houses built in the fifties. Sidewalks, alleys, normal working people. I came up fine.

When I opened the door she showed me a mealy grin and said she was here about the room for rent. Does it matter if she's good-looking? Imagine her however you want: big eyes, high cheekbones, wet lips, whatever, then throw in some little flaw so you can believe she'd actually materialize before the likes of you. Her teeth in front were too short—stunted and gray. I said I didn't have a room for rent. This was one I hadn't heard before.

The Olsons' former black lab, Dooley, came vulching toward us and the girl hugged herself closer toward my door. I shooed him away no problem, but he glanced back at me in an insulted way, as if to say there'd been some big misunderstanding and he belonged indoors. All of them gave you this look at first. Eventually they got over it, forgot about who they'd been.

The girl was pointing at her car along the curb for some reason, like that qualified her as nondesperate. Then she showed me her little notebook where she had my exact address written down and the word ROOM in big black letters, as if that verified everything.

"From an ad in the paper," she said. As if anybody reads papers anymore.

"Maybe you got the address wrong?" I said.

At this point the average conniver would start asking for something, trying to touch my arm or call up some tears. But she just nodded, like she was used to getting things wrong. Her mouth moved into a funny cramped-up position and she couldn't look at me. She turned and headed back to her car, which was filled to the ceiling with stuff.

"Shit. Hang on." You never know. You never know about people. There might be one in three telling the truth now and then, and what kind of asshole do you want to be in the final tally? I grabbed my keys and my coat and we headed down the street a ways, looking for a ROOM FOR RENT sign on a block of empty houses. Before we turned the corner I glanced back, fearing some crew of guys with crowbars would pile out of her car. But nobody did.

"Was there a phone number in the ad?" I said.

"Just sunny and clean was all it said." She said her name was Molly. She said she was a good roommate, clean and considerate, and then neither of us said anything for a while. She had pulled up the hood of one of her sweatshirts so it was hard to see her face as I walked alongside her. With her fists jammed into the pockets in front she looked more or less like any regular hood rat I'd known in high school.

Most of the houses had big posters in the windows with two huge eyeballs and the words, THIS HOME IS BEING WATCHED, but we all knew that wasn't true. Folks had started scavenging them, breaking out the back windows and pulling out appliances and copper plumbing in the night.

"Why would you want to move here?" I said.

She made a noise I couldn't decipher.

After a while, looking around at the houses, she said in an awed and mystified voice, "It's like missing people."

"Sure, like a fucking zombie movie," I said, maybe too meanly, and she got quiet again.

Dusk came along and slipped in around us. We walked up to Old Aggie's house over on Elm, and her holiday lights were on bright as a construction zone. "Maybe here?" I said. She compared Aggie's address to the one in her notebook. "I don't think so," she said.

I could feel Aggie shuffling around behind the door, wondering about us. "It's just me, Aunt Aggie. It's Tommy." She wasn't my aunt but that's what we called her. She opened the door bundled in a red robe over her regular clothes, like St. Nick. She knew everything about everyone in the neighborhood but she hadn't heard about any room for rent.

By then it was fully dark out, though it was only 5:30 or so. Fucking December. We kept going, approaching every house with lights on, but no dice.

On our way back to Molly's car I said, "Might be that somebody placed the ad and then had to move away sooner than they thought."

"You stayed put. Why haven't you moved?"

"Ours is paid off."

"You live with your folks?"

I didn't say anything, just shook my head in the dark, where she couldn't see it. "I grew up here."

There in my front yard I had a déjà vu to my first date, with Malgosza Gombrowicz, Old Aggie's granddaughter. It was Christmastime, every house gaudy with reindeer lights, and I walked her home and we stood in the middle of her front yard, which was shaped just like mine. She was staring at me with her big bulbous blue eyes and leaning in with her lower lip hanging when her dad opened the front door and spooked me, but I went ahead and kissed her anyway. That was big courage, back then.

In this girl's car there were sweaters in laundry baskets, grocery bags bulging with CDs. A bundle of crumpled sheets with a hairdryer on top.

"How much did the ad say the rent was?" I finally asked.

There's one thing I didn't mention before, because I didn't want to come off as some creepy self-righteous douche. The truth is, before Molly showed up that day, the truth is I was praying. It's not like I do it all the time or anything.

I didn't like the idea of putting her in my dad's room. I hadn't enshrined it or anything, but his stuff was still pretty much the way he left it. His shirts were hanging in the closet, his socks and underwear folded up in the top drawer, his workpants and t-shirts in the big drawers underneath. In the nightstand next to the bed, I knew, were stacks of *Playboy*s arranged by date, unwrinkled. And pinned on the walls everywhere were his little quotation cards, things he'd made from scraps at his printshop on slow days. HELL IS OTHER PEOPLE, and NEVER HURRY, NEVER REST. That sort of thing, letterpressed into thick pastel paper left over from somebody's wedding.

I got a couple of laundry baskets and started packing things out of my room, putting them into my dad's closet. I stripped the sheets off my bed and stacked a fresh set on the desk for her. It was a small room, and I didn't need everything in it. I hesitated about the stereo, then left it for her.

"OK," I said. In the front room she was sitting in my dad's reading chair, staring out the dark window to the yard, where the Jacksons' dog, Mabel, was staring back.

She said, "You won't hardly even know I'm here."

The house was about nine hundred square feet. I was pretty sure I'd know exactly where she was.

She made her way to my bedroom, a little warily. I stepped back so as not to crowd her. She looked around, gave the mattress a squeeze. "OK then," she said.

The stuff in her car wasn't exactly what you'd call packed; it was more just thrown in there piece by piece, so we carried it into the house best we could, leaving a trail of items across the lawn and down the hall to her room—a Red Wings sock, a half-eaten Snickers, a Radiohead CD. When the car was about half empty she said, "OK, that's probably enough stuff," and she locked it up.

"You hungry?" I said as we walked inside.

She looked surprised by the question. "No. Just tired." She went in my room and I waited, but she didn't come out.

That night in my dad's bed I rode out my usual ambush of night fears, but now there were new ones related to this girl. I imagined her going from house to house each night, nestling in and then stripping your place clean and driving off at dawn in that packed-tight car. An anti-Santa, relieving you of your attachments. But then I heard a soft cough on the other side of the wall, and a while later there was a yawn and a creak of the mattress. My mattress. She was falling asleep like anyone, filling the house with her breath, her real life. I slept like the dead. I dreamed my mother came back. She came knocking at the window and I got up and pulled her in, scraping her stomach on the sill until we tumbled down in each other's arms. It was eleven years since I last saw her but she hadn't aged. Her hair was still the same black flapper's mop. She said, "Your father has finally stopped harassing me with his phone calls. What happened?" And I gave her the rough outlines of his demise. She listened without much reaction. I screwed up my courage to ask, "So will you move back, now that he's gone?" But I could see her retreating even before I finished the question. So I closed my eyes to stop seeing her that way and I dozed off in her arms and dreamed another dream of her, a better dream inside the first one. We were floating over the city in a hot air balloon looking down at the lights and the big dark holes where lights used to be, over the vast, abandoned central depot and down Michigan Avenue toward the old heart of town. She was a great explorer and I was her navigator. Her hair flew up around her face and she leaned over the edge of the balloon's basket, giving me a look so bright and intense it was like she had just given birth, and I gasped and grinned back at her until she said, "Don't you have anything bigger than this to dream of?"

So I did what I knew she wanted me to do: I climbed over the edge of the basket and jumped, and woke up. It was like I'd been infected by my dad's pillows and taken on his fever dreams from the very end. And I felt pained for him all over again, if that was the kind of dream his last dreams had been.

The house was quiet and bright by then so I got up and stumbled toward the bathroom door, which was open, though it shouldn't have been, because inside, there was Molly. Sprawled in the bathtub, naked and gone. The water was cold. Her mouth hung open. She was like something washed up on my shoreline.

There was no blood anywhere, just a few pill bottles floating in the water, with my dad's name on the labels. I dropped to my knees and squeezed her wrist, waiting—fuckit, praying. In a way, every body is the same in the end, cool and lackluster, abandoned. "Goddamnit," I said. "Too much, goddamnit." And finally I felt it, like a worm swallowing something under the soil: a pulse. I put my cheek near her mouth and felt the faint sour whiff of her breath. OK, then. OK.

Step by step. I let out the water, threw some towels over her, and went to find the phone. The 911 lady let it ring a long time and then asked in a skeptical voice if this was an emergency. When she heard Molly was breathing, she lost even her meager reserves of urgency. She said, "If you can get her to throw up, that'd really help us out."

On TV the operator stays on the line until the emergency crew shows up, but that didn't happen. This woman seemed to have someplace to be.

I kneeled down next to Molly, waiting. Her skin was clammy and cool, blue gray. I lined up the empty prescription bottles and tried to remember which ones had been for the chemo, which ones for the pain.

Then finally a low, funny moan came from some great subterranean distance, and she moved.

"That's right," I said. I made all kinds of retarded cheerleading remarks. "Come on now, you can do it. Let's go, Molly."

"What'd you do to me?" She came to life. "Oh, fuck, it's freezing in here."

So I carried her into my dad's room. She was piled in towels on top but still naked and wet underneath. It was like picking up a strange furry animal and discovering its slick, heavy underside. I set her in my dad's bed and piled all our spare blankets over her. I brought over the garbage can and asked if she could find a way to throw up. "I'll get right on it," she said.

I gave her a t-shirt, sat down on the edge of the bed. "I called the paramedics."

She rolled her eyes. "I'll be fine."

They probably wouldn't come anyway. "What were you thinking?"

"What were *you* thinking?" She was still slurring her words from the drugs. "Who lets some stranger into their house? What exactly were you expecting?" She said it in a leering way that set me off.

"What if you died here? In my house? I mean, fucking go next door if you want to do that."

She went big-eyed and quiet. "I thought about it."

A big angry weight collapsed through me like a live demolition. She tried to patch it over, take it back. "I didn't plan it. I just saw those little pills and wanted to try them out. I didn't want to die or anything. God."

I shook my head. "Who *does* that?"

"I do," she said. And then at last she started throwing up. The sound and smell of it was so familiar I felt myself shrivel up and sneak out. My body kept holding the garbage can for her but the rest of me was someplace else, staring at one little card pinned up over her head that just said SOLVITUR AMBULANDO and nothing else, and I wondered what it meant or if it could be a guy's name and if so, who that would've been. There were all these mysteries now that no one could answer.

After a while there was nothing left in her stomach and she was seized up, gagging out yellow bile. I got her some water and she lay back. Her face was red and teary, strained like a balloon.

She said, "Don't you have to go to work or something?"

I was keeping his printshop alive on my own now, but nobody much would notice if I opened a few hours late or not at all. So we sat together against the headboard, just breathing. A light snow started coming down outside and I think both of us dozed off for a while.

"Maybe we should take a vacation day," she said, which woke me up. "We could turn up the heat real high and make sugary drinks."

"OK," I said. I had nothing against it.

"I want to go someplace really hot, you know? I want to go someplace where it's sunny all the time."

"You should."

"Shit," she said, like this was the equivalent of going to the moon.

She closed her eyes for a while and I thought she'd dozed off again. I sat watching the snow. My legs were falling asleep and my tailbone ached. I was considering sliding out of the bed when she said, "Hey, for real, can we turn up the heat real hot, just for this one day?"

I got up and flushed away her puke and turned the thermostat to seventy-nine. Underneath us, the furnace whirred into motion with great purpose, like it had finally been called upon to fulfill its dreams.

"Hey, it's snowing," she said. By now there were already a

couple of inches on the ground. It had even covered over the hole in the Wozniaks' roof.

I thought of something my dad used to say. "Snow is the one thing the movies have never gotten right, and therefore haven't yet destroyed." He was prone to grand claims like that.

She smiled and sat up straighter to get the full view of it. "Yeah, that's true."

We watched it coming down in its weightless way, turning the whole back yard and alley into some kind of dream. I wanted to help her somehow. "Anybody you want me to call?" I said, but she wouldn't answer. "Anybody you believe in?"

She made a sound like wind rushing through her teeth.

"Me neither," I said, which was just about true. The praying had been only an experiment, and look what it yielded.

A pair of little dogs started yelping at each other in the alley and Molly said, "I'd like to do something for those goddamn dogs, before I go."

The extra heat brought a funny new set of smells to the house, a kind of festering mushroomy jungle quality, and it really did start to feel like we were on vacation someplace exotic. The landscape outside was powder-coated and muffled, totally uncorrupted by shovels and snowplows. We sat at the kitchen table eating sandwiches and staring dumbly out, and I knew that one way or another she was going to vanish as abruptly as she'd arrived. And even if she didn't take anything at all, I'd spend the rest of my days going from room to room trying to figure out what was missing. But for now she was just making chewing noises and shifting in her seat, making plans.

Her idea for today was to break into the old homes of all the dogs I recognized and let them go curl up and sleep in their old beds, out of the snow. At least for the night. She said, "Don't you think that would quiet them down a little?"

I didn't answer.

She wanted to start next door. "While you rustle up Mabel by the collar I'll climb in the back windows and open the door for you. I'm good at this," she said.

"With the snow we'll leave tracks," I said. "From our house to theirs. It'll be obvious who did it."

She said, "It's kind of sweet how you still think anybody cares."

I went back to my sandwich, thinking it over, and she went on trying to convince me. A real hopeful look came over her face, like she was imagining that those houses inside still looked like they used to, with couches and chairs, and bowls of dog food on the kitchen floor, and beds with blankets and pillows, the whole place warm and dry. She was right that the dogs would be overjoyed at first, unable to believe the world had finally heard their appeals and decided to put things right. They'd race through the door barking, "Honey, I'm home," and scramble on their long, unclipped claws from room to room. They'd go hunting for traces of their lives, finding foul new smells and wires exposed and puddles from burst pipes. Big empty spaces where the beds had been. They'd start making those panicky high-pitched noises and they'd look back at us, perplexed and answerless, all of us realizing together that we had no solution at all for this. We knew nothing. I knew this because I'd already tried it before.

Family Planning

INSTEAD OF THE gold-plated onion domes Josie had hoped for, the view from their room revealed only the grimy, cement backside of the Oktyabrskaya metro station, where a few merchants had set up tables selling flimsy newsprint magazines bearing pictures of naked women. She held her map of Moscow up to the window, trying to match the city in her head with the one hulking in the half dark outside. "I think we're *here*," she said, stabbing at the map and looking over her shoulder to Meg. "I think the river is that way."

"I don't want to go out," Meg murmured. She was suffering theatrically on the narrow bed by the wall, with her red hair splayed across her face and her arms tightly coiled around her slender frame.

They should have been happy. They were here; it was coming true. But Meg had gotten sick on the airplane, and their first Russian meal—cabbage and kasha and some kind of fried cutlet—was gurgling around in their stomachs.

Josie paced along the wide window. "Maybe some fresh air . . ." she said, but stopped herself. There was no sense being difficult. In their eight years together, she didn't recall ever winning a dispute with Meg. Still, there was so much to see out there, and they only had six days. She pressed her face against the cool window and practiced sounding out the few simple words she recognized on the dozens of bright city signs—КИНО, УЛИЦА, КАФЕ, МЕТРО. Meg had refused to take Russian lessons with her, claiming it was too hard a language to be able to learn anything useful in only six months, but Josie had gone ahead and taken the lessons anyway. It seemed important to try.

"I think I'm going to be sick," Meg moaned.

"Sshhh. They'll hear you."

To reduce costs the adoption agency had arranged for them to stay these few days in an apartment with a host family, and the walls were thin. Josie could hear their hostess, Sana, humming along with the radio in the kitchen as she cleaned up after their welcome dinner.

Josie sat down on the edge of the bed and smoothed Meg's hair off her face. "You want to go to the bathroom?"

"There are cockroaches in the bathroom."

"Don't be a wuss. Every city apartment has cockroaches."

"Not ours."

Josie decided not to tell her that occasionally, in the middle of the night, she'd seen a lone cockroach or two scouting their kitchen sink in Chicago. "That's because ours is a condo," was all she said.

Meg flopped onto her other side and pressed herself against the wall. She was being childish, but Josie let it go. She had romanticized this trip pretty elaborately in her mind, had imagined them holding hands and grinning nervously: future parents. Abroad. In the homeland of the mystery child who was waiting to become theirs. She curled up behind Meg and put her cheek in the hollow between her shoulder blades. "We could just walk around the block?"

"Give it up," Meg said, but Josie could hear she was smiling.

"You'll feel better tomorrow."

"God, I hope so."

In the morning they would drive west, to an orphanage outside of town, which the Russians called a *baby home*, where they would see the boy with their own eyes.

"And then, just imagine—"

Meg stopped her. "You said you wouldn't get your hopes up like this."

"I'm not."

"You are." Meg stretched out her legs, effectively pushing Josie off the bed. "I'm sorry." She shifted to make room for Josie again. "But you have to keep in mind all the things that could go wrong."

Josie crossed the room and sank into the other little bed beneath the window. For months now Meg had been enforcing restrictions on their optimism. No plans, no painting the spare bedroom, no shopping for clothes or car seats. Not yet. Josie told herself this was just the businessperson in Meg, the part of her that believed that if you made your desires public you would get screwed by everyone. She brokered deals for a big real estate developer for a living, scooping up and pawning off office buildings and industrial parks. It was a world of poker faces, where nothing turned out as it seemed.

"Don't pout," Meg said. "Please."

"Well, we're here, aren't we? Hasn't everything gone just like the agency promised?"

"Wow, they picked us up at the airport. Wow, we've been sheltered and, let's not forget, *fed*. Remarkable. Let's sign our lives over."

"You act like this is some elaborate con, like all of Russia's conspiring to take your money."

"Our money," Meg said.

Josie pressed up to the window again and watched the strange little cars racing by around the corner. A whole world of Russians was out there, and she might never get out and meet any of them.

"I just want to protect us," Meg said after a while. "You."

She was right, of course. Even if the agency did everything perfectly, they would still have to wait months before coming back to pick up the child, and there was an awful lot of potential for failure along the way. The boy's health might be too problematic, the courts might not approve the deal, or he could get whisked away by any Russian couple stepping in at the last minute. And then there was the strange possibility that they might meet the boy and somehow, somehow . . . not feel the right thing.

"Sometimes," Josie said, "you've just got to make a leap."

A brittle knock came from their bedroom door, and Josie realized that after all her studying she didn't even know how to say "come in" in Russian. What good was she? She walked over and opened the door to find Sana's daughter, Natasha, struggling under the awkward weight of a large tea tray.

"Chai," the little girl said, her face twisted up with effort.

"Come in, come in." Josie rushed to clear a space on the desk for the tray.

Natasha began a flurry of words in her beautiful, singsong voice, but Josie understood nothing. At last the girl reduced her comments to one word, enunciating it over and over. "Sakhar? Sakhar?"

Josie and Meg looked at each other, baffled, until finally Josie thought to say, "Spasibo."

With great ceremony Natasha put two spoonfuls of sugar into each small cup and poured tea to the brim. Then she smiled and launched into more incomprehensible prattle. Josie thought it sounded as though the girl was asking permission for something, and they nodded, thanking her again and again. Finally she gave up and opened a drawer under the bookcase to retrieve two ragged Barbie dolls and a handful of crayons, seeming to apologize for invading what was now, temporarily, their space. Then she excused herself and rushed out the door.

"This must be her bedroom," Josie said. They looked around at the drab, fuzzy wallpaper and the tidy, sterile surfaces everywhere. There were no traces of children's things, no toys or primary colors or drawings tacked up on the walls. Everything was brown or forest green. But in the corner by the window, under a folded blanket, they discovered a wooden cradle so small and feeble looking that it had to have been made for dolls.

"That's got to be a toy," Meg said.

"I should hope so." Josie pushed at it gently, and it rocked to and fro with an uncertain, antique creaking.

They stood staring at the tea, suddenly dazed and tired beyond words.

"You want to push the beds together?" Josie said.

Meg stepped out of her pants and folded them neatly over her briefcase on the desk chair. She gestured toward the door, toward the family beyond their rented room. "I don't think we should."

Josie watched Meg undress and tuck herself into the bed until she became only a faint lump under the covers. She tried her own matching low, narrow bed, but her feet hung over the end and her arms flopped down to the floor. She felt monstrous in it. She lay still for a while, pressing one palm against the low mound of fat between her navel and pelvis, where she could feel the grumbling machinery of her digestive tract and, underneath that, a faint, premenstrual throb.

Finally, unable to sleep, she got up and fished the adoption agency's handbook out of her shoulder bag, then sat leaning against the window to catch the little bit of light from the streetlights. The cover of the booklet featured a black-and-white image that Meg had dismissed long ago as embarrassing: an adorable, gender-ambiguous baby in nothing but disposable diapers, crawling innocently across an artfully rumpled American flag. The pages that followed told little of the immense bureaucracy and expense of it all, of the social worker visits and weekend classes, the thousands of dollars spent with no guarantees, the fear and doubt and growing desire filling these many months. The book was promotional, devoted to testimonials and photos of satisfied customers. The husbands and wives in these stories had great posture and carefully ironed clothes. They thanked the Lord. They were certain the kids they brought home—*miracles, gifts*—would know nothing but health and prosperity in their new world.

When they'd first gotten the booklet in the mail, Josie and Meg had smirked at these pages, feeling daunted and excluded by the strange confidence of those parents. "We're not going to do this matching Disney outfits thing," Meg had said, pointing at one family photo. "That's not mandatory, right?"

Over time, though, Josie found it hard not to get swept up by the pictures. The stories, the babies, pierced through her skepticism, made her previous life seem small.

She glanced over to make sure Meg was still sleeping, then pulled from the pages the snapshot they had been sent of the boy, their boy. Nikolai.

His eyes were small and set far apart, divided by a nose that seemed uncommonly flat. It was hard to get perspective on him, since he was posed alone in the photo, but he seemed small. That was common, they'd been told. He weighed, they said, only fifteen pounds, at eleven months. He wasn't standing up or walking. He wasn't smiling. He was sitting in the corner of a metal crib looking away from the camera. The neck of his t-shirt hung low, revealing the ridges of rib bones across his upper chest. Josie ran one finger along them, wanting to plant baby fat right there.

"You know," Meg startled her, "I wish you wouldn't get so attached to him yet."

Josie closed the book guiltily. "I know. I know." But she didn't need to look at the picture anyway. The boy's face was wallpapered inside her mind. She had sketched backdrops behind him too: Nikolai under the Christmas tree; Nikolai in the bathtub, surrounded by boats; Nikolai asleep in the car seat with a bottle tight in his mouth.

What she liked about these images, too, was the picture of herself and Meg they implied: focused, permanent, purposeful. A family was a thing that stretched out beyond where you left off.

The following morning their guide, Artur, came by after breakfast to take them to the orphanage. He was a tall, pockmarked young man who spoke excellent English, each phrase perfectly enunciated, as if there were a computer in his bulging throat stringing together separately recorded words. He helped them collect their paperwork and their bags of gifts for the orphanage, and they said good-bye to Sana and the little girl and headed downstairs in the narrow, dimly lit elevator. In addition to the agency fees and the three thousand dollar "donation" to the orphanage that were itemized on their Good Hands bill, they were advised to bring gifts for everyone in Russia, including the kids at the orphanage. They had fulfilled this charge dutifully, stuffing their suitcases with diapers and clothes, toys and baby formula. This was how things got done in Russia, they were told.

What they didn't understand, though, was how and when to offer the gifts. Did they pull out a sweater right now for Artur, or give it like a tip upon departure? Either way, it smacked of condescension.

Artur had a rickety little red car that was inexplicably missing the front passenger seat, so Josie and Meg sat together in the back, tensed up and wondering at everything they saw. They careened through the crowded streets of Moscow, swerving and screeching to a near stop every time they encountered another pothole or obstacle. Josie was relieved to find that not all the buildings were like the mysterious gray, Soviet-looking behemoths she'd seen from the apartment window; many were beautiful old stucco buildings, painted pale yellow and burgundy and pink, with elaborate porticos in front. The sidewalks were wide and crowded with people, and on every corner there seemed to be little makeshift markets with piles of fruit and vegetables. When Josie aimed her camera at them, she realized that at the edges of the markets stood rows of people holding out dresses and coats for sale, their arms spread wide like scarecrows. She took a blurred picture. Within a few minutes they were on a bridge over the Moscow River, and off to one side, in the distance, the gold domes of the Kremlin churches shimmered in the sunlight like a fantasy.

Artur offered to take them to Red Square, and Josie nodded eagerly, but Meg cut her off. "We *will* meet the baby today, right?"

"Most likely," Artur nodded casually, without looking back at them. "If everything goes well."

Meg's face turned hard and masklike. Josie had seen this

transformation whenever Meg took business calls at home. She seemed ready to launch into an offensive strike, but Josie squeezed her hand. And, surprisingly, this subdued her.

Artur outlined their schedule for the next two days, explaining the process of "approving" the child and putting the paperwork in motion. If all went as planned they would come back in six to ten weeks for a final adoption. The six-to-ten-weeks part sounded like a mail order promise. Josie tried not to dwell on it.

Artur wasn't paying much attention to her anyway. He addressed all his comments to Meg, only glancing at Josie from time to time out of politeness. Meg was the official adopter, after all. Russian law didn't give kids to gay couples, so although they would both become legal parents in the States, in Russia Josie was supposed to pretend she was merely a traveling companion. It had been easy to agree to this in theoretical terms, before the trip, when it seemed she could sacrifice anything for a baby. And Meg's life looked much better than hers on paper: She earned three times as much as Josie. She had a long history of stable jobs and residences. It was because of her savings that they could afford to do this at all. What judge would look at Josie's résumé—a slew of brief, poorly paying jobs followed by eight years of toiling on an art history PhD that she was beginning to admit she might never finish—and grant her custody of a child? She couldn't even conceive one—six miscarriages in two years. Her failure seemed written across her forehead. She understood why the adoption had to be done this way, but on the ground now, this role of silent partner, secret parent, chafed at her: Meg, the official parent, when Meg had to be talked into all this.

"It's nice that you came to help Meg," Artur said to Josie, maybe picking up on her distress signs. "This can be quite a difficult time."

Josie smiled wanly back. She was a terrible liar. Meg had said it was all merely formality, that obviously the people in the Russian agency would see them for what they were. Only on paper, in front of the Russian judge, would they need to uphold this lie. But now, with Artur's gaze upon her, Josie didn't feel so sure. A silence fell over the car. She took back her hand and shifted her thigh away from Meg's.

"We've been friends since childhood, like sisters," she announced suddenly, lying. "We met at summer camp."

Artur nodded up at the mirror and smiled again. "Do you have children yourself?"

"Not yet," Josie blurted, then glanced with panic at Meg, feeling she'd turned the conversation all awry.

"Do *you* have any kids, Artur?" Meg asked quickly.

"Not yet." He winked. Josie didn't know how to take it. He seemed slightly effeminate, but maybe that was just how Russians were. A silence settled over the car, and in time they passed from the downtown streets on to the smoother, more orderly highways leading out of town. Josie sat quietly, trying not to imagine the orphanage, hoping it would take a very long time to get there.

She had read the Human Rights Watch reports. She had seen

pictures and documentary films of twisted, forlorn babies lying half naked on plastic mattresses. The photos showed cold metal cribs lined up in rows, almost like cages. She had seen one film about an orphanage that had no electricity and sometimes even lacked heat and running water. The children, even the healthy ones, were said to be dazed and indifferent for lack of interaction. They were rarely held; they might not know their own names. Some of them would have even given up crying.

The agency's booklet said nothing about these things, except to mention in the back end of a paragraph that some children might suffer from sensory integration disorder or have difficulty making the transition to a "forever family." And maybe it was true; maybe Human Rights Watch reported from orphanages much worse than those near the capital. Maybe the steady feed of adoption money made this orphanage heaven compared to the rest. That's what Josie told herself as they moved farther from the city and off onto quieter, narrower country roads. She watched the green fields and forests rushing past the car windows, the little dachas appearing in clusters now and then. Every so often Artur would point out some landmark or tell them which famous Russians had houses nearby. But before she felt ready, the car slowed down and turned onto a rutted dirt road, approaching a small guardhouse. There was no one inside it to stop them, so they drove past.

At the end of the road, beyond a few withering shrubs, stood a building that had once been pink but was now faded to white near the top and saturated with gray filth along the bottom. There were grates on all the windows, and no traces of children in the yard. No swing sets. No bicycles. The entrance stood under a small portico, held up by four large, peeling white columns, and in black letters above the entry hung the words ДОМ РЕБЕНКА. Baby home.

Artur got out of the car; Meg and Josie stayed frozen in the backseat.

"Well, this is it," Meg said, feigning ease.

"Yeah," was all Josie could say. The air around her hummed.

They collected their bags of gifts from the trunk, shouldered up their purses and video camera, and mechanically followed Artur up the stairs. Inside, the foyer was austere and clean, with high ceilings and deeply worn parquet floors. The air smelled of cabbage, and there seemed to be no one, no voices, no sounds, anywhere. Artur went down the hall and came back a few minutes later with a short, heavyset woman wearing a white lab coat over her dress. She led them to a large office, where Josie and Meg set down their bags and waited. The woman collected Meg's dossier of documents from Artur, and sat studying them at the desk for several minutes. Josie started to worry. She nudged Meg and glanced at the gift bags.

Meg nodded. "We have these gifts for the orphanage."

The woman held up her hand to quiet Meg.

When she finished with the documents she said something to Artur that surprised him. "Apparently," he said, translating, "they actually have two children who are, ah, eligible for adoption, that you can meet today."

Two children. It struck Josie suddenly as incredible good fortune: two children to choose from, not one. There was an abundance. But glancing at Meg's already dismayed face, the implications sunk in: How did one choose between two children? And what about the little boy in the photo? Was he one of them?

Meg said, "I can only afford to adopt one child."

"Of course," Artur said. "Of course. But if you would like to meet them both—"

"Is that common?"

Artur shrugged.

To be summoned across the ocean to meet one desperate boy seemed almost a heroic mission. To sit in an office and have babies paraded for your approval was something else. A shopping trip.

Meg made hesitant, disapproving sounds, but then she consented. The woman went out into the hall with Artur and they were left alone waiting for a long time.

"Maybe this—" Meg whispered.

"What?" Josie hissed back, trying not to lean too close to Meg. She had the unlikely sensation that they were being watched.

"Nothing."

"Tell me."

"Could this have been a bad idea?" Meg's eyes were flashing from side to side, scanning the bare walls.

"It'll be okay," Josie said. "This is natural. I mean, the nerves."

"But what if—"

The door opened and the woman in the lab coat came in, walking backward to hold the door with her shoulder. In her arms, they realized as she turned, was a baby. No blanket, just a gray sweater and tights, and a shock of coarse, platinum hair.

It was seated in the crook of her arm, and when it saw Josie and Meg, it neither cringed nor smiled. It glanced at them with vague disinterest, then let its gaze land on the blank wall behind them.

"This is Sveta," Artur said. "She is seven months." Josie stood up, then remembered her role as bystander and nudged Meg forward.

"Hello, Sveta," Meg whispered at the baby. She was very tiny; Josie would have guessed she was only three or four months old. The woman jiggled the baby a little, trying to make her smile. Instead, the baby lunged at Meg's red bangs and clamped on, pulling them back and forth with a ferocity that stunned them all.

"Ostorozhno!" The woman slapped Sveta's little red hand away, and Josie braced for tears. But the baby just stared back, revealing nothing.

"It's OK," Meg said, trying to hide her alarm. She leaned forward to let Sveta take her hair again if she wanted. But Sveta drew back, and then lost interest entirely, staring at the wall again.

Josie stepped into her line of sight. She was wearing a dark green sweater with white trim, and the baby stared at the contrast in colors for a long time but wouldn't look at her face.

"Hi." Josie nudged one finger against Sveta's fist, waiting for her to latch on. "Privet, Sveta!"

Sveta looked from one person to the next without emotion.

"Look at her little eyebrows," Meg cooed. Josie took away her finger, for the baby refused to grab it.

They smiled and waved; they made funny noises. They shifted Sveta around from knee to knee, bouncing her, tickling, rubbing her warm, knobby head. They didn't think of head lice. She smelled very clean. She seemed, in fact, flawless but for her indifference. They took pictures of her, and then they got to the business of the videotape. They'd been advised to video the child and show the tape to a pediatric specialist at home. There were certain behaviors, apparently, that might reveal something important. Josie and Meg didn't know exactly what to look for. Sveta's eyes moved in tandem when tracking objects, and though she didn't respond in any way to her name, she seemed to notice sounds around the room. The woman in the lab coat demonstrated this, going off in a corner behind Sveta and making different noises—clapping, whistling—to illustrate Sveta's response.

"She has some mild hearing loss in her medical records," Artur explained. "But you can see that she hears quite well."

After a while they took Sveta away, and Artur and the woman went over the baby's medical records with them. She had tested negative for hepatitis, syphilis, and HIV. She had been suffering from malnutrition when she first arrived, but she had plumped up nicely since then, they thought. They offered no information about her birth parents.

"If you want to," Artur said when they were done, "you can also meet the boy, Nikolai."

Meg sighed. "It feels like a lot to take in."

Josie put down the video camera. The picture of Nikolai was just inches from her feet, in her purse. And somewhere, beyond that thick, sterile door, he was off in a crib, in his thin pajamas, waiting. The girl had seemed perfectly fine, it was true. She would be good enough for anyone. But Nikolai, Nikolai, Josie felt obliged to him.

"Maybe you should at least see him," she said. "While we're here. I think you should meet him." She tried to sound casual—*just a travel companion*—but her eyes fixed on Meg desperately.

"I don't know." Meg looked away. Josie sat helplessly in her separate chair, nearly two feet away. "Maybe—could we meet him tomorrow?" Meg said.

Artur talked with the large woman a moment, then nodded his head reluctantly. "It's possible," he said.

And they began to shuffle together the papers, to collect their things as if the visit were over.

"Wait, wait," Josie said to everyone, wishing she could remember the Russian word for this. And then, though she knew they would all hear her, she whispered, "I think you're making a mistake."

Artur glanced from Josie to Meg and back again.

"We still have tomorrow," Meg said to Josie. "This is all very overwhelming."

Josie widened her eyes at Meg, then covered her mouth with her fist and said, in a rapid mutter she hoped would be difficult for the others to decipher, "If you do this to me . . ."

"OK," Meg said at last. "OK. You're right. I'd like to see the boy."

The woman in the lab coat seemed disappointed, as if she had already gotten used to the idea of being done with them for the day. She sighed and shuffled heavily out of the room. They sat waiting with Artur, not saying anything. After twenty minutes, through the silence they heard a baby's cries coming closer and then receding, muffled by the voice of the woman trying hard to calm him down.

At last the door opened. He was clinging to the woman's shoulder, clenching up and then kicking his little bare legs in her arms. She turned around so they could see his face over her shoulder. It was flushed and distressed. He stretched his neck up as if fighting to get free, then dug his face into her shoulder to hide. There was no other way to say it, he was writhing. "This is Nikolai," the woman said in heavily accented English.

He was scarcely bigger than the baby girl, although they said he was eleven months old. His hair was red and wispy, growing in splotches. He wore a dingy cotton onesie with no diaper underneath, and had little pink plastic sandals strapped on to his feet.

The woman bounced him against her shoulder awhile and Meg hesitated, then reached out and touched his back gingerly, as if she thought he could hurt her. "Hi, Nikolai," she whispered. "I'm Meg."

"He's adorable," Josie said to Artur and the woman. "Krasivyi," she said, trying another Russian word.

Meg gave her a funny look. The boy was not adorable. The skin on his arms was pale and grayish, and it was difficult to tell whether he was dirty or this was just his natural state. Josie didn't care. She stepped up and took him. All concerns about acting her part fell away. She didn't care what any of them thought. This was her boy.

And he went to her, clutched her shoulder and chest as if she were the vortex of a spinning nightmare. His chest heaved against her with a raspy, wet sound. When she leaned back to get a look at his face it was anguished and red, in need.

"Tikho," she said. "Quiet. It's okay." But he wasn't crying. He was just struggling without tears. His body was hot and soft, and Josie realized that, like Sveta, he smelled unlike any other baby she had ever held. There wasn't a trace of Johnson & Johnson's on him.

The woman smiled and chuckled a little. "Maybe you each found baby," she said. "Maybe you want him?" she asked Josie.

Josie glanced at her only briefly, then closed her eyes against Meg's gaze. She wanted to be alone with the boy. She thought she felt his muscles relaxing into her body. She had no idea how long this took, or if she might have imagined his calm or only grown accustomed to his struggling, but by the time she remembered Meg again and turned to look, Meg wasn't where she expected. She wasn't standing nearby watching, taking pictures or video. She was over by the window, staring outside at the empty, muddy courtyard.

That night at the apartment Meg played dolls with Natasha for a long time after dinner. They spoke nonsense to each other, giggling and bumping the battered Barbie dolls along the coffee table in different imagined scenarios. Josie sat at the small kitchen table with Sana, drinking tea and looking through a photo album at vacation pictures from Sana's trip to the Black

Sea. The jet lag was getting to her, and she and Sana had long ago exhausted their limited vocabularies in each other's language, but still it seemed hours before anyone decided it was bedtime.

At last, alone in their room, Josie said, "So, what did you think?"

Meg yawned and turned out the light. They lay down in their separate, narrow beds, with all of Natasha's toys well hidden around them.

"I think we should sleep on it," Meg said.

"No," Josie whined playfully, trying to pace herself and keep the mood light, because she knew how much lay ahead of them. "I mean, he's a redhead like you, Meg. And petite. Think of the pictures." She was stooping to Meg's basest weakness for perfect appearances.

"I have an idea," Meg said.

"What?"

"Let's let the doctor at home make the call. We'll show him the video tapes and their medical records, and leave it up to him."

Josie was quiet.

"I mean, on the one hand, she has the hearing deficiency—"

"You know that's no big deal," Josie said.

"Well, maybe."

The boy, on the other hand, had some sort of issue with his stomach, they'd been told. This might or might not have been the cause of his discomfort today. He was older and thinner and more complicated. He had spent more time in bad hands, as they said. There could be other problems lying in wait, of course. But wasn't that true of any child?

"You're just saying that because you know the doctor will choose Sveta."

"We don't know that."

"Just be honest. I mean, if you want the girl, you should just say you want the girl."

Meg didn't respond for a long time. Then she said, "I think the doctor will know best. Will be impartial."

"You're saying I'm not."

"How could you be? How could either of us be?"

Outside, a car alarm started wailing. "*You* seem to be pretty impartial," Josie said. "You know what else? So is that little girl."

"What's that supposed to mean?" Meg said.

They had the same cool insulation of indifference, Josie thought. She'd be surrounded by them. Across the room, in the strange light, Meg's profile looked foreign, unfamiliar. Josie wanted to be the kind of person, for once, who could insist on something at any cost. But she just listened as the car alarm cycled through its various warning songs. So this was how it would go, she thought. A stranger would enter their lives, muscle in, take up residence in the rocky, dangerous, delicate space between them.

"She's just, she didn't have any . . . emotion. It was spooky."

"Listen," Meg said in a peacemaking tone. "I don't think we should say things like this about *either* of these babies. Either one of them could become *ours* very soon."

Josie's insides swooned at that comment. Finally Meg had allowed the possibility.

For a few soaring minutes Josie let herself think about nothing at all. When her thoughts drifted back they had turned against her, grown tentative. Maybe Meg was right, she thought. Maybe it was best for a doctor to take this decision off their hands. Wasn't it normal to wish for a healthy baby? Wasn't it agony to watch a child suffer?

The ideas twisted around inside her. She thought of the car being burgled outside, of its windows smashed and its dashboard gutted. She thought of the owner, the thief, the assaults of the world. She thought of the baby boy's parents too, who could be out there as well, maybe thieves, maybe homeless, maybe buried underground in a place she would never find. "But, you know," Josie said very quietly, working her way back to the surface, "if we don't take him, who will?"

Meg sighed, though not in an unkind way. She understood, Josie thought; she felt the weight of the choice. She was just trying to be practical, to protect them. Josie heard the rustle of blankets, and then Meg was beside her, pulling back the covers and climbing into her bed. She weaseled her cheek into the crook of Josie's shoulder, and Josie had to hold tightly to Meg's back so that she wouldn't fall off the edge. Comfort. She was coming to comfort her.

"The thing is," Meg said, "this is the rest of our lives we're talking about."

And Josie realized in a cold flash that all this tenderness was being applied toward Meg's interests. She realized that this was how deals were made, by measuring risk against potential and probing the other party's capacity for compromise. Meg was good at this; she was a specialist. Someone had to give, sooner or later. This was how families and lovers everywhere functioned. It was not just a business thing; it was a kindness people gave to the ones they loved. Josie told herself to stop thinking now, not to cry, not to ruin the illusion that the choice they were about to make would be mutual and fair. Because if she said it aloud, if she admitted, even in this small public space, that she was willing to sacrifice this desperate, unknown boy for the pleasure of the woman she knew best and nevertheless loved, she would never be able to take it back and hide it away and be swept up in the inevitable feeling she would find for this Sveta, this Sveta who would become their world.

GOD OF FIRE

"I'M SORRY, IS this awkward for you?" the man next to me says at last. We're in the back row of a DC9, leaning close to hear over the engines.

He's been telling me how his next-door neighbor once had an aneurysm. She was mowing the lawn at the time; her death was nearly instantaneous. "I mean, is this a good distraction?" he says. "Or would you rather I leave you be?"

"It's fine." I shake my head and smile. In the numb efficiency of panic I have already told him about my father and the call from the hospital chaplain that set me in motion today from Detroit to St. Louis. "I think I would *sense* something if he"—the flight attendant bumps past us in the aisle—"died," I say. "Died. I think I would feel that."

He nods and looks into his drink. It is possible he thinks I'm devoted to my father.

I scan the gray air outside, opening myself up for that sensation you always hear about. Does a part of me—however vestigial—feel torn away, missing? It doesn't. My father is a fierce, invincible giant. Death has come to him three or four times already, and each time he's sent it running.

But when I see him, when I make my way from the airport to the hospital, down all the winding corridors to his bed in the ICU, I think surely this is it, this is his last life. His body is swollen and rosy, drugged unconscious. He looks as though they've filled him with too much blood.

Tucked into the small space between the ventilator and the bed, my mother clutches his right hand with both of hers.

"What do the doctors say?" I whisper.

She's afraid to move her gaze from the EKG monitor over his head. Every rise and fall of that jagged line assures her: He hasn't died, he won't be diminished, they'll be back home in no time. "They don't know, Ellie," she says. "It isn't good." She is barely five feet tall, one hundred pounds. He towers over her in real life, as do I. "I just know—" She shakes her head and closes her eyes hard. He is her only monument. "I just know he's going to end up like one of those *people*," she says, "dragging an oxygen tank around with them everywhere."

The adult part of me wants to prepare her for eventualities, to remind her of what the hospital chaplain told me: Almost no one survives a ruptured aneurysm in the aorta. But the child part stays quiet, knowing how expert she is at bending the truth to make things go his way.

There's a chair in the corner but my mother won't sit in it, won't take a nap, so we stare at him, side by side, all through the night. Swaying, feeling my head go tingly, I count the tubes threading life in and out of him, and speculate on the world beneath his eyelids. I think, even now, he can't fathom that he's weakened, that he could just sputter out and die like an ordinary man. Instead he dreams bold, kaleidoscope dreams, sees visions twisted by morphine and trauma. As the night chugs along, I imagine he gives himself over to these fantasies, so that the sight of the doctors with their knives and needles fades from his consciousness and he finds himself wholly elsewhere, someplace warm and sunny and festive. It's the tropics, I think, Mexico or Costa Rica, with the swoosh and salt of the ocean just out of reach. The temperature and humidity are too high, unbearable; the resort is low-budget, with monkeys in the treetops. From his lounge chair on a crude stone terrace, high in the hills above the ocean, he writhes and sweats and curses his travel agent. "What kind of a joint are you running here?" he shouts to no one, to everyone.

The kindly hippie couple who appear to be in charge refuse his requests for cocktails and cigarettes and keep telling him, "Take stock. There will be a group meeting at eight."

This has the air of a therapy camp or cult, some sort of rehab facility maybe, and he recoils. "I'm parched, for Christ's sake!"

"Now Mr. Kernes," the hippie woman scolds, stooping to push at his pillow before leaving him. She is dark haired and curly and widest at the middle. She wears an orange flowered muumuu that gets caught in the crack of her ass as she walks away from him.

"How about a newspaper at least?" my father yells at her backside. The woman shakes her finger in the air without looking back, and then descends the steps of the terrace and disappears. Down on the beach, in the distance, a little girl squats over a pile of sand, working. She has dug a moat near the waterline that is three feet deep and stretches to the horizons. My father shifts in his chaise lounge and wishes someone would wipe his brow. He has been told to watch the ocean for signs, but his insides are rigid for lack of nicotine and he cannot move his arms.

"Hold his hand a minute," my mother says to me, "so I can blow my nose."

I step closer and put my gaze hard on him. I have never held my father's hand. The fingers are swollen big as sausages and hot to the touch. His arms, tangled with IV tubes and monitors, are strapped down on the bed. All around him the machines vibrate and hum, suck and push, bringing his chest up and down. I think of placing candles on his palms, of setting a little bell on every finger.

By morning I've made friends in the waiting room. It's a big open space, with room for twenty or thirty devastated people. The chairs—aqua-blue vinyl recliners—are clustered in small groups and rows to give the illusion of privacy, but the room is crowded today so I am forced to sit with strangers. To my left is Neil Hartman, a grandfatherly sort, who is on his forty-first day here watching his wife, Nancy, die of cancer. He is tall and gray haired, slender with worry; he walks as if he's just finished a marathon. They've been in and out of this hospital for several years now, and Neil knows which buttons to push on the phone to get an outside line. On the other side of me is John LaPointte, whose wife, Lorrie, is paralyzed from the waist down after enduring the same kind of accident, as he puts it, "Princess Di died from." I'm too afraid to ask what he means by this. He's goateed and portly, thirty or so, and tells me he teaches gym class to high schoolers for a living, mainly so that he can keep on coaching football. We sit in a row, with our chairs kicked back, facing a television hung from the ceiling.

Neil says, "So you're the triple-A miracle everyone's talking about? That's your dad?"

"I guess so," I say, and since they keep looking at me I do my best to explain my father's surgery. I tell them how his aorta dilated to eight centimeters from the aneurysm yesterday and then burst, spilling pint after pint into his abdominal cavity. "It's right along here," I say, running my fingers down the center of my stomach. "I always thought the aorta was in the heart, but it's more than that, apparently." Neil and John nod as if they've been learning anatomy too. "It's like the main river of your body."

"And they fixed it?" John shakes his head. "Son of a gun."

"Like an inner tube," I say. Then we return our silent attention to the TV, where the constant flow of news reassures us that horrible things happen to everyone, all the time, all over the globe. Behind us, the coffee maker spurts and hisses, and a can of pop bounces down the chute of a Coke machine. I don't tell them we're waiting for my father's kidneys to fail, or that his lungs are filling up and he's hot with infection. I don't tell them there are blood clots shooting around his body, that they have gone to his leg, that they could still go to his brain.

On CNN, golf legend Payne Stewart's private jet has gotten a mind of its own for some reason and flies ever northward, upward, into the cold, dry atmosphere above South Dakota. Two Air Force planes follow behind at a distance, ready to shoot it down if necessary. The announcer says it must be on autopilot, that the bodies inside are surely frozen by now. I picture their oxygen masks dangling from the ceiling, just out of reach.

With the enormous duffel bag weighing him down, it takes my father many hours to descend the rocky sides of the terrace. It doesn't seem right that he should have to escape a tropical resort, but it's dream logic he's following, and dream instinct tells him those hippies and their therapy talk are going to spoil any chances for fun on this vacation. As he climbs down he stops several times for air, wishing for a cigarette. By the time he reaches the beach it's nearly dawn, and the monkeys are racing from tree to tree back into the forest. The little girl, still digging in the sand, squints across the beach at him. "Mister," she calls, jumping up. Her face is filthy, and from the knees down she's coated in sand. "Hey, Mister."

My father turns from her and starts walking up the beach. There has to be a town somewhere eventually, a normal resort, a cantina.

"Hey, Mister." She trots along in his wake.

"No comprende."

"Where you going?"

He stops and wipes his face with his hankie. "For smokes." The duffel bag has grown larger; the strap is tearing the skin from his shoulder. "Where's a store?"

Now that she has his attention she smiles coyly. "A store?" She slaps her plastic shovel absentmindedly against her belly.

"A store. Cantina." He puts two fingers to his mouth as if to inhale. "Cigarettes. Cerveza."

"Want to see my moat?" She squints up at him. Her cheeks are full and sunburned. Her dark hair blows up around her head in all directions, like a fire.

He sighs and shifts the bag to his other shoulder. The contents are heavy and jagged as bricks.

"I'm in a hurry." He starts walking again, faster, focusing on the sand. Dozens of iguanas scramble out of his path.

"I dug it special for you." Her voice comes at him from all sides, otherworldly.

He takes off. She struggles to keep up with him, diving for his ankle.

The bag digs into his other shoulder. "Fuck off!" he shouts, kicking loose of her easily. As her body flies through the air it shrinks smaller and smaller, receding like a hummingbird, a fly, a gnat. She's gone.

With a shudder of revulsion he hurries away, hoping no one has seen this.

....

My mother is going to the chapel for Mass and wants to leave him in my charge. "Visiting hours don't apply," the nurses say, "in cases like this."

"Everyone's so nice here," my mother says, genuinely charmed. She doesn't seem to notice or care that they bend the rules only because they have no hope for us. Her mind has room for only this thought: He has lived twenty-four hours longer than anyone expected. And for this, for whatever slippery, back room deal she worked out with her God last night, she must pay tribute. "I'll be right back, Tommy." She kisses my father's hand, smiles up at him, blinks, and wipes something off his forehead. Then she surveys the urine bag hanging under the bed and pushes aside the curtain to leave. "Talk to him," she says. "They say he can hear us."

But I never could talk to him, never could hold his attention. To do so now, with him captive like this, would seem like cheating. And what would I say? "These antics of yours, will they end soon, will they ever?"

My father has always been the loudest voice at the party, the luckiest man in the casino, the widest grin at every ruthless joke. He eats with abandon, drinks every day, and even after his bypass surgery last year continued to go through two cartons of cigarettes a month. In my twenty-six years I have seen how intoxicating he is to his friends and how savage he can be to the rest of the world. As the person who made him a father, I was born to the wrong side. The death of the party, I learned to sit quietly and watch.

So I stand here obediently, feeling the heat rise off his body, wondering where the real Tom Kernes has gone. With its tangle of tubes, its whir of ventilation, this broken thing in front of me is more machine than man, yet still it sweats, it throws off energy. I extend my hands, palms out, over his belly.

Would I say, "I search every man I meet for what you wouldn't give me?"

The nurse charges in, and I draw back. She wants to check on his legs, which are wrapped in long vinyl inflatable cuffs. A machine at the foot of the bed inflates them in sections, then releases, inflates, releases, pushing the blood up and down through his legs. She puts her stethoscope on the top of his right foot. "Hi Mr. Kernes!" she shouts, and I jump. "Just checking your feet!"

Leave him be, I want to say to her, or he will make you sorry.

"Yeah, this one is colder," she says to me, tapping his left foot. He doesn't wake or stir. She rolls in an ultrasound machine and rubs some gel on his left foot, then scans it for a pulse, for anything. There's a blood clot in his thigh, they think, cutting off circulation. "Can you feel that?!" She slaps at his foot and shouts, "Mr. Kernes, can you feel that?"

I glare at her. "It's OK," I say. "You can leave him be."

"Wake up! Mr. Kernes, come on!" she shouts.

And it happens, his head stirs, his eyes open. He comes to life before us, a giant tied down. I shudder and step back, gripping the chair behind me. The machines wake up too, in a chorus of beeps. His blood pressure flashes impossible numbers: 213/165, 224/173, and he writhes, eyes searching. "You're in the hospital, Tom," the nurse shouts, nearly smiling, and I wish her dead. He blinks and gags, rips his head side to side. Where is my mother? Why can't she take this from me?

I level my gaze, fighting the urge to run. "It's me, Dad."

His glance flickers wildly from her face to mine. I am no one, anyone to him. His arms are strapped down so he kicks, shifts his body.

"I'm here, Dad. It's Ellie," I say. I put my hand on his arm and squeeze. His mouth gapes and clenches at the tubes down his throat, and I can feel the muscles knotting under my hand. I won't cry here, never in front of him.

The nurse unwraps his next dose calmly. I can see him straining against the pain, but even in his confusion he knows this is a weakness to be hidden. He turns his gaze to the fluorescent light over his head, blinking into it, gnawing fiercely on the ventilator tube, until the morphine hits. Then he brings his eyes back to mine for a moment of lazy, dazed blinking, and in that half a minute it seems he's trying to remember me. Against my better judgment I find myself wishing all over again that he would see me, that he would linger on me. Instead he sinks down into his dream world like a fish heading for dark waters. The nurse snaps off her gloves and leaves without saying anything.

I sit down on the chair and press my palms to my eyes. I squeeze the sides of my head to keep things in. When I look up, a Mexican woman in pink scrubs is mopping the floor around me. "Don't get up," she says. "You're all right."

I say, "This is my father."

She nods and smiles, then works her way gradually out of the room.

I push down the bed railing and lean over it so my forehead touches his sweat-soaked sheets. "Hi Dad," I say into the mattress. "It's me. Hi." I pause and search my brain. "It's pretty outside," I say at last. "The leaves are changing."

The machines hum and beep.

And so I decide on a lullaby, something he always sang to me. "*I don't want her, you can have her, she's too fat for me . . .*"

In the waiting room frail old Neil is making a scrapbook of press clippings, recording the news of the world for the wife he is losing. She has always been addicted to newspapers, and Neil is sure she'd hate to miss out on any developments. His sister-in-law is here too now, carrying her Bible everywhere, even to the bathroom. These are the last days; no one can really believe Neil's wife will see another remission. But we can't just do nothing in here.

"How about this one?" I say, tearing out an article about the apartment bombings in Moscow.

"She'll like that," Neil says. "Thanks." His scrapbook has a page for each day of this stay, and the cover, when closed, rests at a forty-five degree angle.

Scratching his goatee with hesitation, John hands him one about Al Gore and Bill Bradley in New Hampshire. "How's this?"

Neil nods and thanks him, but puts the clipping off to the side.

"A Republican, eh? I'm sorry." John's smile astonishes me. Yesterday I heard him say *brain damage* to someone over the telephone. One moron in a pickup truck can steal half his wife's brain and body, and he still thinks to tell my mother that her sweater matches her eyes.

MSNBC interviews a man in New York who was trapped in the elevator of his office building all weekend with nothing but a roll of Life Savers and six cigarettes. They have set the camera up in his living room, because he's too traumatized to leave the house now. He may file suit.

Walter Payton dies.

Shellfish are floating up in the Gulf of Mexico.

I'm afraid to leave the bubble of this hospital, and I'm not the only one. John has borrowed his brother's camper and parked it at the back of the parking lot so that he never has to go home.

My father's doctor wants to speak to us in his room. When we go in, the leg cuffs are off, and the doctor has drawn two lines on either side of my father's left shin. "Put your hand here," he says, but my mother backs away like a spooked animal.

I step up and put my hand there on his leg. It is hard as a baseball bat.

"It may be," Dr. Lessario says, "that the muscles are just so swollen that they're forming a kind of tourniquet here." He runs his pen over the blonde hair on my father's calf. "In which case we'll just make two vertical incisions here to ease that pressure." This is the best-case scenario; he offers it only to pretend there is hope. We believe him. The other possibility is that the tissue in his leg is already dead, is already poisoning the rest of his body.

My mother folds her arms and nods, inhaling. They'll be cutting away at him tomorrow.

"Cerveza." My father raises his empty bottle. He is free of the hippie resort at last, and has found a reasonable spot on the beach, where people are laughing and eating. "Una más."

The waitress pulls a pen from her hair and nods without making eye contact. As she heads to the bar, he watches the back of her dress, the sway of her hips. When she opens the refrigerator, several bright green lizards rush out and scatter across the floor.

At the next table three surfers and a shady local are playing poker. It is night inside the bar, smoky and dark; little white lights are strung along the tented ceiling. But there are no walls, and outside the sun is high, and the sand's too hot to walk across. My father wipes his face with a coarse napkin. Somewhere out of sight a heavy metal can drops through the workings of a pop machine, and he's thirsty. "Whew," he says to the surfers. "It's a son of a bitch out there."

They tilt the light over their table to shine it in my father's face. "You want something?"

"No." He shrugs. "Christ."

"Just kidding," the smallest surfer says. He looks no older than fourteen, but he has silver caps on his front teeth and a bowie knife in his lap. "You want to play?"

They each have fifteen or twenty cards in their hands and car keys on the table.

My father is the luckiest man he knows.

"You got a car?" the tall one asks, pointing at the keys.

"One better." He pulls his chair to their table, working from a memory of something he maybe once had. "I've got an airplane."

Outside an old, dark-skinned woman in a pink outfit walks her cow along the beach, with a long rope tied around its neck. The weather is shifting; the wind kicks up and inflates the woman's loose shirt like a sail.

They cut off his leg today and put him on some new kind of sedatives so he won't stir toward consciousness again for a while. While he slept, while he dreamed, they cut off his leg, and if he wakes up, we're going to have to explain what we've done to him. At 2:00 a.m., unable to sleep, unable to keep my eyes for too long on this new shape of his, I go out to the parking lot because there's supposed to be a meteor shower. But the lights everywhere make it too bright to see anything, so I go around to the back of the hospital, hoping for more darkness. I climb up on a cement retaining wall at the darkest part of the lot and nothing shines above me, but below me a ramp leads down to the dumpster area. They have different colored dumpsters for hazardous and non. They make a lot of garbage here each day, and I think, is it in there? Is it in that one, or in that one?

"Hey risk taker," John's football-coach voice booms from the ground beneath me. "You ought to come down from there."

I can see his cigarette glowing in the night.

He climbs up next to me and we sit hanging our knees over the cement wall without speaking. "Neil's wife died." John rubs his hands over his large stomach, smoothing his sweater down. "I thought you'd want to know." Behind us, on the other side of a wooded patch, the cars rush down New Ballas Road, where even at this hour people have places to be in a hurry.

I think of her scrapbook, of all the useless news clippings. "Oh." I can't find any words. "Oh, man."

He nods. "She fought hard."

"Yeah." The pavement around the dumpsters is littered with scraps. I think of old Neil driving home alone, stopping at all the yellow lights in caution, pulling into his driveway and into his empty bed.

"How's Lorrie doing?" I ask.

John shrugs, then pauses and shrugs again. "They say she'll go to a regular room soon."

"That's great news."

"Sure it is."

"Do you not want to talk about it?"

"Nope. Nope, I do." The meteors have started bursting overhead, laughing down at us. "Today she pointed at me."

"Yeah? That's good, right? That's good."

He nods, then points at the dumpsters. "It stinks over here." He lights another cigarette and looks skyward. "I could really go for a drink."

"I hear that." The wind gusts through my hair, and a thought occurs to me. "Hey, wait. Come with me."

I pop the trunk of my parents' car and shove my father's golf bag aside. The sight of his paired-up golf shoes knocks all my breath out. I step back and shake the thought from my head, then push them deep into the recesses of the trunk. "Here." I pull out a six-pack of Miller Lite. "My father's stash."

"Lord have mercy," John says. "Where's that lady with the Bible?"

We sit on the bumper of my father's Cadillac and the beer goes right to our heads. When John was seventeen, he says, he inherited his grandmother's '67 Eldorado. "Sky blue," he says. "Big as a house inside. Lorrie and me took it all the way to Alaska at ten miles to the gallon."

He tells me he's afraid to drive his car now. It's not the other people, he says; it's not the common, easy fear of winding up beside or behind the wrong driver. It's him, he says. It's the thought that with one dumb slip of the hand he could kill someone. "Or worse."

I realize I'm staring at him, mouth gaping. I close it, look away. I understand.

He shifts and shrugs. "What's your dad like?"

I would like to tell him that my father tucked me into bed at night and took me for bike rides. That he taught me to fish or smoke or mix drinks, that he knew my nightmares or at least my phone number. But he didn't. I rub my eyes. "He liked to burn things."

John sets his beer down dramatically. "What?"

I sip my beer through a smile and nod. I have what can be a funny story. "He burned up a car once."

"A car?"

"Well, not to the ground or anything. But he tried. He would have liked to. It was a lemon."

John's laughing now, so I tell him about the Ford Country Squire wagon with bad timing when I was eight, and the country road at sunset and the gas-soaked rags my father kept throwing on the burning carburetor. I tell him about the kind little man who pulled over and ran across the road with his fire extinguisher and how my father shoved him away and glared into the fire, declaring, "Just let it burn."

I don't tell how I cowered against my mother in the ditch, crying, waiting for the explosion I feared was imminent. How I wished she would stand up and stop him. How when I asked her, years later, what had happened that day, she said, *Nothing. What fire?* She couldn't remember a fire. And I knew then I was alone and she was not to be trusted. *The station wagon? I don't know. I think we sold it*, she said. But my memory of that day in the ditch was firm: Her eyes were riveted on my father and those flames, which kept dying out anyway amid all that metal machinery. It must have thrilled her to know that a man that wild, that untamed, had chosen her and stayed so long beside her.

I tell John, "After that my friends and I started calling him the God of Fire." We would tower over any item of frustration, sentencing our broken toys and dolls: *Let it burn.*

"You mean, like, what is it, Zeus?"

"We didn't know Zeus from Moses," I say. "At that age."

I tell John about the bonfires he used to build, big as sheds, and the fireworks he shocked the neighbors with every year, and not just in July. I describe his great, suntanned, muscular form squirting lighter fluid onto dwindling campfires, chopping down dead trees, burning boxes and magazines, anything paper, while grinning like a delinquent into the flames. He had a great booming laugh I could hear from any hiding place.

"God of Fire." John chuckles. "Tom, is it? Tom Kernes, God of Fire. It's got a ring to it."

I nod. It does. I don't tell how once, near the end of a party, he picked me up by one hand and foot, swinging me around and around in dizzying arcs toward the bonfire. I don't describe my fine white little-girl hair ripping through the dark like a torch as he shouted over my squeals, *Should I throw you in the fire, Ellie, should I?* I don't mention the liquor-sweet scent of his breath or the panic gripping my heart as his hand slipped and I wet myself, begging him to spare me. And that laughter of his, that crazy, infectious laughter working so hard to prove that this was fun.

"It's Prometheus, I think," I say.

John touches my knee. "The gods don't die, Ellie. They almost never do."

You fucked with the bull, puto." A man named Arturo plunges a final kick into my father's stomach. He has no wallet to take, no car keys, no airplane, of course, so they have beaten the lesson into him. He writhes on the ground and groans until they lose interest and leave him alone on the beach. He's been slashed down the middle and is wet there, and the inside of his mouth is raw with punches. He feels himself falling away from it all, losing hold in the dark, but then shakes himself awake. They are twenty feet away when he gets to his knees to dig into his pockets. He finds the long strap of the duffel bag in there and pulls it out length by length, coiling the strap beside him, until with one last tug the canvas bag pops out, much smaller now, but just as heavy as before.

He stands up and begins swinging the bag high over his head like a lasso. With every turn it grows larger and larger, and he lets out the line until the bag whoops through the air like a great vulture bearing down. Arturo and the surfers hear the noise at their backs in time to turn and face it, but too late to duck. They are caught full-on in one swoop. The bricks scatter free of the bag on impact and ricochet off their skulls and jawbones, off their shining teeth. The canvas bag drifts to the ground, deflated, but the bricks sail off, bloodied, high into the sky. One strikes an electric line before falling. It makes a quiet *pop* and sends a shower of sparks into the trees.

My father limps over to the bodies and rifles their pockets for cigarettes. In the tree above him a family of spider monkeys has gathered to see about the commotion. They dance through the limbs, chattering angrily, casting their minstrel faces down at him. "Whooo," the big one says.

My father inhales deeply, looking from the bodies to the monkeys and back again. He casts his match down at the tree roots. "Fuck you and your mother."

He stumbles down the beach away from the bodies but tires before long and stretches out on the sand with his head in the weeds. He is bleeding. He has lost a lot of blood, and his insides are mangled. The waves crash in nearby, and he blinks at the heavens, thinking there might be an airplane flickering above. "Hey," he moans, raising one limp arm to wave. "Down here." He smiles and shakes his head.

He awakens to the smell of smoke and the crackle of brush fire. The air is ablaze, and the weeds along the beachline catch fire. He wants to run, but he can't find his feet, and his belly feels ready to split open if he moves. The monkeys are screeching, but there are no people anywhere. Finally, with one hand holding his stomach in, he gets to one knee and pushes himself up to stand.

A tug from his leg pulls him down again. There's a rope tied around his left ankle, he sees, and at the other end of the rope is a little girl, a different one, fatter. "I'm helping you," she says. "Come on." The fire is right at his back, burning his skin.

But every time he tries to get to his feet she tugs at the wrong moment and trips him again. "Goddamnit!" He summons his last strength to coil the rope between them and yank her off her feet. He pins her thick shoulder into the sand and gets up. He manages a few steps toward the ocean, dragging her.

"Hey!" she says, laughing. "Hey, knock it off!"

He falls again and can go no farther. They're only a few yards from the moat she has dug, and beyond that the ocean is very near. She leans against the rope like a bargeman. He holds his side and watches the muscles in her legs straining. They move. With each step she grows larger and stronger, so that when they reach the moat she just bends down and cradles him up, crossing the moat in one stride and bringing him right to the waterline. She lays him down in the shallow water where the waves tug and push his body. She is tall as a house over him. The saltwater stings, but she says this is good. "The fish will clean you out."

The World Series is over.

EgyptAir flight 990 goes down off Nantucket.

Microsoft is declared a monopoly.

Neil is gone; there are new people in his place. There is never a shortage of faces here.

John comes by now and then to say hello. His wife has been moved to a regular room on the third floor, and sometimes I see them in the courtyard: she, strapped tight to her chair, her chin squeezed convulsively against her chest, and he, shuffling behind her with nothing but a cigarette. She seems unable to speak or understand, and he doesn't introduce me. "So sad," my mother says, unaware that worse things could happen to us still. We are worn down, tatters of our former selves, grateful for things like water, like air.

"Do you remember the time," she says to me one day while we're watching my father's body, "when you spray painted flowers all over the side of Dad's car?"

"No way." I blink at her. "You're making that up."

"Hardly." She snorts. "You were a handful, always trying to goad him."

It seems impossible that I could have blacked out a transgression as big as that, but I close my eyes and, after asking her which car, which color flowers, I imagine myself in our old garage, shaking the rattling cans and squeezing the trigger. It comes back:

the aerosol smell, the cramped hand, my own vicious chuckle. It was a brand new Buick Riviera, black. I had offered to help him wash it earlier that day, and he'd responded with nothing but a booming, "Don't touch." She isn't lying.

"How come you never reminded me before?"

She shrugs. "It was done, I guess. Sleeping dogs."

So now there is nothing for me to be sure of. All my memories seem faulty, invented like dreams. The man before me bears no resemblance to that towering one in my mind. This one, the flesh one, on day twenty-eight now, has begun to wake up regularly. A piece of clear tape covers a sore on his right ear. His mouth is free of the tube now; they have cut right into his trachea. When he slips down in the bed he pushes with one heel and wrestles from side to side until he works himself back up toward the pillows.

"See how strong he is?" My mother smiles. "You're so strong, Tommy," she shouts into his ear.

But he ends up skewed, lopsided on the bed. And the skin hangs loose from his forearms, the muscles wilted. The stump of his leg, wrapped tight in ACE bandages, snaps high in the air, as if astonished at its sudden weightlessness. His one leg is still wrapped in the inflating cuff; the other cuff dangles under the bed, inflating and deflating around nothing. He is a fraction of my father, powerless to terrify. At long last, after so much resistance, I'm ready to learn my mother's skills; I'm ready to give the benefit of the doubt.

When he sleeps, when no one is looking, I can run my fingers through his soft, white-blond hair. When we ask if he'd like us to swab his mouth, he stretches his jaws to the limits like a nested bird, hungry for any small thing.

And when my mother leaves the room for Mass I remain here, teetering above my father, dreaming his dreams for him. Every now and then he pushes the air extra hard through the tube in his throat and seems to be struggling to speak. The doctors say this is good; this is progress. He may come off the ventilator soon. "What is it?" I say, pushing my ear against his stubbled cheek. He wheezes and strains through the tube, needing something, and between us a long life of uncomprehending silences stretches its arms out and yawns.

He falls back, exhausted, pointing his taped-up fingers at the air in some vague gesture.

"What is it?" I prod him again, ready to start over from zero, amnesic. I push at his shoulder and shout, "Just say it!"

But he flashes his eyes so violently I know I've gone too far. I whisk my hand away and he relaxes, making an almost smile. I can see him relish, like a child, the small satisfaction of having controlled me.

It is a small thing. I kneel down next to him, and quietly, so as not to provoke him, I ask, "What do you want from me?" What else can I do?

ЦАРИЦЫНО

In our Russian culture textbooks this is the night when everyone pours into the forest and stays out till dawn jumping over bonfires and searching for magical fern blossoms. The girls are supposed to put messy wreaths of flowers on their heads and dance like sprites in loose peasant dresses, then find some body of water and set their wreaths drifting off with their wishes. It's called Ivan-Kupala, all of this, which means John the Baptist, according to Amy. What John the Baptist has to do with ferns or fires, nobody knows.

Yet when we come out of the metro and onto the street, nobody else in the crowd heads toward the forest. Most people trudge the other way, toward the blocks of identical high-rise apartments, their arms thick pendulums swinging their loaded bags. It's ten o'clock but still light out. The days here stretch long, like fantasies.

Vadim's in the lead of our group and says to hurry up. The two bottles of vodka in his string bag clink together as he lights his cigarette. He knows the way. Sasha has pickles and a bottle of moonshine. The tall, silent guy with the broken-apart face has a soccer ball and some black bread. Andrei, who keeps bumping into me, has a bag full of shashlik meat that's been unrefrigerated since morning. What I've got is a bottle of orange Fanta and the bedspread I stole from my dorm room, which has bedbugs.

From the station to the woods it's a long walk past shuttered kiosks on a crumbling road to a big park that has a few festering ponds in front. Rising on a hill beyond them is a sparse, dusty forest—dark wood, not birch. There's a half-built castle in there somewhere, an abandoned palace called Tsaritsyno. Or so they tell us.

"This place used to be called Black Mud," Amy says. She did a field trip here on her last study abroad.

"No," says Andrei with great certainty. But then, "Is that true?"

"Didn't John the Baptist get his head, you know, taken away?" I ask in my cockeyed Russian, but nobody knows. The Americans shrug; the Russians look at me like I'm a religious zealot. Andrei leans in and whispers a question about swimming, about water. "What?"

He tries again, breaking it down for me: "Did a priest, so to speak, put you in the water and say a prayer over you?"

Was I baptized. "Oh. Yes. But I was a . . . kid," I say, groping for the word *baby*, until I remember they don't really have a word for baby. Or for thumbs. I rock an invisible small thing in my arms to illustrate.

He makes that thrilled grin they produce when they learn something exotic about us. We do it to them too.

There are eleven of us—five American girls, six Russian guys, all of us college students in Moscow from elsewhere. The Russians are Soviets, actually, from places like Tbilisi and Minsk and Dushanbe. By the end of the year the word Soviet will be obsolete in the present tense, and their homes will become separate countries. For now it's still July 1991, still perestroika. Still empty stores and lines around the block and murals shouting WE'RE BUILDING COMMUNISM!

"Is this holiday about the . . . most long day?" Jane says, then asks Amy how to say solstice. *Solntsestoyanie*, it turns out. I repeat the word in whispers but an hour from now it'll be gone.

Andrei and Vadim make some kind of joke that even Amy only half understands. She confers with them, then translates for us: "They said mostly the holiday has to do with sex, with mating."

"They used the word *mating*?" I say. "How do you say mating?"

Jane, my sweet, sheltered roommate, draws herself inward. Sarah and Eileen cluster away from the guys, bouncing between them a look that says, *Why did we agree to this?*

I just keep walking. The next time Andrei brushes against me, I jog ahead and start kicking the soccer ball forward with the tall, silent, harmless boy whose name is either Edik or Erik or Adik—none of which ever appeared in my Russian books.

The air gets darker deep in the woods, but twilight hangs with us past midnight, until an almost-full moon steps in. I don't see any castle. There are no sprites in the woods, no other revelers, no flowers or glowing ferns. Just the mosquitoes, making noises like portable fans. The boys drop their things and go off to collect firewood, and we, accustomed to their gender divisions, just spread out my bedspread on the hard-packed dirt and wait. We've even worn skirts.

"Why don't they ever have grass anywhere?" Eileen switches to English while they're away.

"Cement and dirt and weeds." Sarah knocks on the ground. "No wonder there's no food. It's the most anemic looking soil on the planet."

"Radioactive," Eileen says, which is their running joke. Amy shushes them, because the Soviets understand this word, and don't find it funny at all.

We're not quite so idiotic at home. Sarah and Eileen go to Yale. We've turned into idiots here, with our broken tongues and perpetual frustration.

I shoo some bugs away from the bag of meat Andrei left on the ground. The guys come roaring back full of purpose and dispute fire-building strategies until at last the flames rise steadily and we can start up with the drinking. They've brought glasses for everyone. They drink only shots and only all at once, in a circle, after a toast. We know this by now. To drink between toasts, or not drink at all, is *nil'zya*. Round one is *To Ivan-Kupala!* Then, *To us!* and *To love!* and *To those who couldn't be here!* The toasts get longer and sloppier: *To the forces of fate that brought our parents together to make us, and the fortune that brought us all together right here!* Eventually we run out of things to toast and resort to *To international friendship!*—which we all shout out sarcastically, because it's painted in big red letters across the lobby of our dorm.

After a while we get hungry enough to swallow the suspect shashlik. We even dig our fingers into a can of oily fish, and then some of the girls go off behind trees to puke. Some pass out; some disappear in pairs; the rest of us wander through the woods and find some ruined fortress walls growing out of the dirt. "It's really true," I can't help shouting, and Andrei, whose broad-shouldered handsomeness suddenly occurs to me, says, "You were doubting?"

It seemed like fairy tale stuff—the magic ferns, the wishes, somebody commissioning a whole palace way out here in the middle of nowhere. And then looking it over and saying, "Nah, tear it down. Rebuild it. No, that's not right either; let's just abandon it all and go live somewhere else." When I scramble up onto a broken wall Andrei and Vadim go wide-eyed for a second, like I've just climbed onto a crucifix. But then they glance around giddily and decide to join me, and Amy and Jane and the quiet boy follow along. His face is like two different faces sewn together down the middle. "So it was Catherine the Great that was build this?" I say, and Andrei says, "No, I think she's the one who tore it down." Someone else says, "I thought her crazy son did something." The guys look to Amy for verification, but even she can't remember the truth anymore.

Somewhere around 3:00 or 4:00 a.m. we put together a soccer

game inside the walls, and it's bright enough to see the ball just fine. We find no glowing ferns, no flowers, and our bonfire dies out before anyone remembers to jump over it. By dawn when we trudge back toward the metro, Andrei's got my hand locked up inside his, and he plants a kiss on me but it's just wet smoke. "Now you're really here," he announces. It feels like the sun never went down, but it must have, at least for a while.

(M) ПАРК КУЛЬТУРЫ

They make the Soviets live in cockroach-infested dorms an hour from the city center, but we get to stay in a brand-new building near the Park Kultury metro station, which is actually all the way across the river from the Park of Culture and Rest Named After Gorky. For some reason we never go over there, though sometimes we walk to the dead end behind our bread store and look across the river at it: ferris wheels, paddle boats, ducks, roller skaters. Tourist stuff, we say. What we do instead is sit in sweltering classrooms bungling verb conjugations. Sometimes we sing songs, children's songs. A lone cat prowls the halls. They show us cartoons.

In our dorm rooms, the radios fixed to the walls above our beds have no ON or OFF switch and no way to change the station—just one bald volume knob that doesn't go down to mute. So we're subjected at all hours to whispers from state radio and the brash static when the signal falters, and the mind-bending *ding dong dong* whenever they want our dim-witted attention. It's hard not to feel we're being watched, being fed propaganda while we sleep. We submit to this, to the paranoic inefficiencies of Soviet life. On a little three-month visit, we can afford to go along, be bemused.

The cafeteria in the lobby smells of fish and boiled fat, and is closed half the time anyway. When there's breakfast it's tea and something like oatmeal with chunks of pink meat mixed in. Some days they are open but have nothing to sell; other days it's alien concoctions like *aspik* and *kompot.* Like most of the people we've met in Moscow, our clothes are drooping and we sleep with our arms cinched around our middles. Like good Communists, we've congealed as a group and refer to ourselves in the plural, always *we.*

Then one morning in August our group leader, Mary, calls us into her room to say we won't be going to class. She's American, a dispirited grad student with compromised hair, who insists on speaking only in Russian to us. But something has happened, is happening, something so grave that she puts the big words in English. Gorbachev is *incapacitated*, or on the losing side of somebody's grab for power. He was scheduled to sign a treaty today that would give more *autonomy* to each republic, but—here she hesitates and throws in some qualifiers—it seems that maybe some hard-line Communists bent on preserving the old Soviet dominance have decided to *depose* him before he could sign the treaty. We're in the heart of the biggest country in the world, with its eleven time zones and fifteen republics, its thirty thousand nuclear warheads. And for today at least, nobody knows who's in charge.

Beyond Mary's window our quiet side street goes about its

business as usual. In slow motion, a grandmother navigates around a vast puddle, clutching a little girl with one hand and a wheeled shopping bag with the other. One boy chases another down the sidewalk. Near the corner, some workers are tamping down hot asphalt with their shovels, which as usual don't seem like quite the right tools for the job.

We're told to go back to our rooms. As foreigners we're special, Mary says, then swaps the word out for *vulnerable.* If she scares us, we'll be easier to watch. She throws in her usual threats to remind us: We can be sent home, we can be failed, we can be picked up by police, or worse.

In the hallway we find Jane just coming in from a jog. She says she saw tanks lined up along Lenínskii Prospekt. How many? She shakes her head, *lots.* A long silence shudders through us.

"Maybe they'll send us home early," Eileen says. She has a boyfriend at home, which has become our collective misfortune.

We go down to the lobby, where there's a shoddy TV, but the only thing coming out of it is *Swan Lake.* Like every other day, there are guards at our door. If our parents could call us we could tell them how very secure we are. How insulated we'll always be from this city, no matter how many burdensome words we learn.

It starts to drizzle outside but we keep our windows open anyway, listening for booms, sirens, signs of change. We think of our friends and teachers and their families, even the guys who sell things by the metro, even the awful woman at the bread store who berates us when we mispronounce things. Like asylum inmates, we lean in to our radios, getting nothing but static and, occasionally, Beethoven. Some of us try to write home, do our homework; some wash clothes in the sink, do sit-ups, clip nails. We wait; we are useless. One of the guys digs out granola bars he brought from home; someone else has M&Ms. We share alike.

Then a French girl from the floor below us comes into our room with wet hair and says we've got visitors. She goes over and leans out our window, waving her arm.

It's Andrei down there, in the courtyard with the tall, skinny boy and his face, his matted black hair. They're huddled together under a big red flowered umbrella. "Privet!" Andrei calls, waving like he's on a ship. He shouts something along the lines of "Let's go see history."

"They locked us under," Jane calls down.

"So what?" Andrei says. "Come out the back way." Jane slowly focuses her big black camera and takes a picture of him.

"The guards," I say.

"I'll work it out," he says, which I guess means he'll pay them off. Andrei, we've discovered, is a *fartsovshik*, a black marketeer, which is why he dresses in American clothes and almost always has money and usually gets what he wants.

Most everyone has filtered into our room. "You guys up for it?" I say to the others, but they just glance at the floor and the walls. Even the French girl says, "No way." With their expensive educations and sculpted resumes, they have real things to lose. I don't blame them. But I'm just a C+ state school kid whose future will be shaped by student loan payments and the vast, jobless Midwest. I might never in my life do anything more than this.

Jane's voice gets very low and anxious. She lost her mother last year but I'm the only one here who knows this. "This is a stupid, stupid idea. You think bad things can't happen to you."

"Bring something to drink," Andrei calls. "I'm really thirsty."

М КРАСНОПРЕСНЕНСКАЯ

Andrei takes my coming downstairs alone as a sign of my commitment to him. When he commandeers my bag and arm I bristle, but there's a bright fear glowing in me so I go ahead and let him take ownership. The skinny boy, Edik, maintains his radio silence as we walk, glancing up only to make sure he doesn't lose track of us. On the Ring Road ahead of us, a lone tank trudges past, as if lost.

Andrei and Edik disagree about where to go. Edik heard people were demonstrating at Manezh Square. Andrei says we should go to Krasnopresnenskaya, head to the parliament building, which everyone calls, with some irony, the White House. For a second they look at me, as if I could possibly know anything. I see two women heading into the metro station with a tricolor Russian flag, not the Soviet hammer and sickle, collapsed between them. So I say, "Could be we follow them."

At Krasnopresnenskaya Station the quick current of the crowd sweeps us past all the bronze bas reliefs of workers and revolutionaries raising flags and building barricades. The only people who seem to notice them anymore are tourists. Every station in town is a cathedral to the worker, the soldier, the revolutionary. Marble columns, vaulted ceilings, chandeliers, mosaics, stained glass. It's a city clogged with monuments. I hold on to Andrei's hand and let myself be pushed and funneled onto the steep, narrow, ultrafast escalator that carries us several stories up from underground. I once heard a rumor about a second, secret metro system that supposedly runs below this one, designed to evacuate the most important people in the event of—here Russians stop the story, because what they were about to say would be impolite—in the event that your country annihilates us with those weapons.

When you're jammed into a thick crowd and you can't feel your feet, it's best to look up, at the chandeliers, and think about the people who built this. It's best not to think about where we're going, or what kind of clashes or crackdowns await us. Andrei twists around to face me on the long ride up. He says, "Don't worry," which is actually, "Don't uncalm yourself." His hand in mine is cool and loose, his posture against the rubber railing as leisurely as a honeymooner's. I turn to see Edik behind me, and he's shaking.

Up at ground level everything's gray and raining, and the crowd clots up again in the confusion of popping umbrellas. Then they wander off in various directions on their separate errands. It turns out there was no surging collective purpose. Most of them don't even stop to consider the line of tanks that's creeping down the street.

"They're all over town," Andrei says, collecting himself after an odd silence. "It's really true."

In Baku last year, Soviet tanks rolled in and killed hundreds of demonstrators. In January, they killed over a dozen in Vilnius.

In '56, as even a mediocre Russian major knows, they took out thousands in Hungary. I think about how I promised my mom I'd be careful. But here I am, unaccounted for, moving toward the parliament building with a growing cluster of strangers. They say Yeltsin's been making speeches to the crowds, calling for a general strike. Edik says, "God, they'll kill him." An old guy near us says, "They haven't even arrested him."

We're quiet for a while, until Andrei says, "I guess somebody cut a deal with someone."

Closer to the White House and the river embankment beyond it, people are dragging junk along the street—metal street signs and construction rebar, garbage and bricks from God knows where. Three teenagers scrape a whole phone booth along the pavement, which incites a roar of approval. The pay phones more often than not don't work anyway. When the boys pause to rest, so many people step in to help them that they get squeezed aside and stand back, laughing as their phone booth moves off without them toward the makeshift barricades.

Across the river, a long, thick line of tanks and troop-filled trucks is inching along Kutuzovskii Prospekt toward us. The roar of them seems louder than it ought to, and the crowd stiffens and goes quiet. "We need more stuff!" a woman yells, and we reanimate: A chunk of people breaks off, looking for more debris. To me though, these flimsy piles of junk look mainly symbolic; even a decent Jeep could find a way around them.

The tanks along the perimeter of the White House sit like turtles, just waiting. The soldiers, poking out of the hatches to smoke, look oddly casual and tired. A cluster of old women gathers around, and one says, "You wouldn't shoot your own grandmother, right?" The boy in the hatch has dimples and red hair and smiles back at her, shaking his head ever so faintly. "You hungry?" she says, and hands him a bag of *bubliki.* He takes it, a little too eagerly.

The crowds dwindle and swell with the rain, so it's hard to say how many we are, or how many there might be in other parts of the city. On Tverskaya, they say, and at Manezh Square, they've overturned trolleybusses for barricades. Some people somewhere, we hear but don't see, have set up tents and campfires, hunkering down for the long haul. Pedestrians on errands make brief detours to see us. They linger at the edges like shy kids near a playground. Some stay, some go. This can't hold.

Then across the crowd I see a woman with her arm up like a Lenin statue. She's waving, which is fine, but at *me.* When I make out her face it's Anna Petrovna, one of my Russian teachers, she of the stifling hot classroom and Cheburashka cartoons. For a second I realize this may mean I'm in trouble, but the grin on her face says otherwise. She winds her way through the crowd to me. "Isn't this strange," she says. "Fantastika." She's pale, maybe forty, with intensely bleached hair and the unrestrained smile—so rare here—of a gold medalist. All our teachers have been distant and formal, but something about running into me here has changed that.

"I'm so glad you're here for this. Where are the others? Take my picture. Take pictures of all of this." As usual though, I forgot my camera. She clutches my arm and from then on we're attached.

Andrei's getting restless. He says, "Let's go get something to drink, why don't we?" We're soaked and chilled but Edik and I hold still. Anna Petrovna dismisses Andrei with a look.

He sighs. "This is just people standing around. Whatever's going on, the real stuff, is going to happen in some back room. A handful of big guys are trading offers right now. This out here means nothing."

An old man near us says a brash three-syllable word to him that I've never heard before.

"I don't care," I say. This out here is all we have. It's beyond curiosity, beyond being barricades or witnesses. Here in this place the abstract idea of collective power is finally palpable. If we go home, and can't even see this on TV, we'll never feel it again.

"I don't think you want to be out here after dark." Andrei gestures toward the tanks. "In the dark they can do whatever they want to you." For a second, a romantic thought flushes through me: If things should go violent, if I should be a victim, would that make the U.S., the West, pay more attention to this? Could I finally, for once in my life, become significant?

A reporter with an Australian accent approaches some men near us for an interview.

"Don't get your picture taken," Andrei says. "Don't talk to anyone you don't know."

"OK," I say. So it's just me and Edik and Anna Petrovna, and a swell of maybe ten thousand people, from a city of over nine million. As Andrei walks away he pauses to light a girl's cigarette, and he listens for a moment to whatever she's saying to him in her beautiful language.

ПРОФСОЮЗНАЯ

The apartment is small, one long, good-sized room. Small kitchen, tiny bathroom, no bedroom. The couch in the main room opens up, and at the far end a single bed is pushed against the wall and covered like a sofa. Anna and Edik help me carry my bags inside.

We open the windows to air the place out and pull open the door to the balcony, which is completely filled with crates of empty bottles and jars.

It's the last day of August and already getting chilly. Anna shows me how to light the stove and boils some water for tea. All the utensils, pots, and pans are here. A bowl of salt and a small jar of sugar. There's even a short little fridge and a telephone.

Edik goes in the bathroom and calls, "Hot water!"

The place is furnished right down to the cluttered contents of the drawers; it belonged to Edik's friend's grandfather, who died last spring. It's forty dollars a month, as long as I don't call attention to myself. No one knows, right now, who really owns the place, or how long it'll take the government to realize that Viktor Sergeevich has died and freed up this little pocket of the state's vast real estate holdings. At this point nobody even knows who the state is. In the meantime, I'm not to talk to the neighbors, not to make noise, not to look like a foreigner—at least not like an American. I'm OK with that. I'm ready for total immersion.

My Russian has improved, but still when I'm tired I get very quiet, which is what I'm doing at the kitchen table while we drink our tea. Anna Petrovna reaches across and clasps my hand like a grandmother. "You've lost your group," she says. "This is a sad day."

We all moved out of the dorm this morning, but the rest of the group took a bus to the airport and I, like a fool maybe, said good-bye and came here. It's been a week and a half since the coup, which lasted only three days, took only three lives. Hardly any violence, for the fall of the evil empire. It's made the world wonder if all our grand fears were invented.

On the phone with my parents last week I tried to explain the job I'd found: translating articles for a new independent news agency. A decent apartment for next to nothing, a front seat to whatever was going to happen here. What was my last year of college compared to this?

"You're not going to turn Commie, are you?" my dad asked, in a voice half joking, half sour. I could hear the TV behind him, the jingle of a local furniture store. "I give her till Christmas," he said to my mom as he handed off the phone. They've always had a habit of letting me drift far, letting me out of their sight.

My mom was quiet for a long time. "It sounds as if you've thought it all out," she said very carefully. Since I left for college, she's taken to watching her grammar when she talks to me. "I don't want to get in your way," she said slowly, and something in me collapsed. I was sitting in a greasy booth in the main post office on Tverskaya, having waited in line three hours for an international phone connection. I traced my finger through the germs on the plexiglass, glancing around the room, where all sorts of desperate-looking displaced people were calling abroad, dying to get there. "You have enough money?" my dad interjected from a phone in the other room. I screwed up the courage to say, "I love you," but my mom just said, "What?" and then our time ran out.

"This is a very green area," Anna Petrovna says. She lives nearby. "Many want to live here. Look at the trees." The building is set back from a busy street, Profsoyuznaya, by half a block of asphalt and pipes and dumpsters. Down in the dirt yard out front, someone has built a homemade contraption for lifting weights. But there are clusters of tall trees all around, and from the fifth floor, if you only look out and not down, you see mostly foliage, and it glows. I try to ask them how to say *treehouse*, but the more I explain the more alarmed they look at the idea of kids living in trees.

"So what happened here, to your face?" Anna Petrovna asks Edik in the sweetest voice, pure curiosity.

He crinkles up his asymmetrical eyes. "Just a little accident, as a kid." His voice is scuffed up at the edges.

Skeptical, she watches him, but decides to let it go. "I have to go now," she says, kissing us on the cheeks. "But I'll come back tomorrow and show you the neighborhood."

Edik and I go in the other room and flop onto the couch, watching in silence as the afternoon sun moves across the room in trapezoids. It lights up the polished dining table, the small white bust of Lenin on the shelf, the dead little TV, the yellowing plastic radio perched on top of it. The dead man's slippers are lined up by the door; his brush waits under the mirror. Before too long, when it gets colder, I'll go ahead and use his bathrobe. I ask Edik how long it's been since he went home to

Tomsk for a visit. He says over a year. I ask about his family, but he just curves his lips into a false smile and shakes his head slightly. His eyes are deep brown and buggy, constant. His nose, clearly broken. His forehead is divided in two by a deep reddish scar that creeps down from his hairline. It picks up again in his pursed upper lip, and again on his throat, near the clavicle. He is a boy who takes you out of the loop of beauty, who makes beauty seem what it's always been: arbitrary and cruel. Imagine a world without beautiful people. There's something thrilling about it. I decide to run one thumb down the middle of his forehead, in that groove.

He rushes in like a middle-schooler to kiss me, as if the chance may never come again. But after a few seconds he pulls back and says, "You feel alone now? Is that the reason?"

It is and it isn't, so I just pull him closer. When it comes to the more perplexing sentiments I'm handicapped by my meager vocabulary, still scared of botching every message. Like him, I've come to appreciate silence and gestures. His hip bones move against me and we're both very thin these days so my hand slips easily up his shirt, down his pants, quick to remove the fabric that separates us.

M ПРОФСОЮЗНАЯ

The country no longer exists, but the city remains. A country is just an idea, its borders only visible in your mind and on maps. But the city is real, noisy and rank, covered in slush and transformed into one vast flea market. Every busy corner or underground crosswalk is jammed up with people selling whatever they can. Against the November cold they hold up blankets and coats, TVs and umbrellas—new products they were given instead of salaries, or old things they've decided they can live without. It's the season of 300 percent inflation and disappearing pensions. The season of eighteen-hour-long nights. The season of *Bush's legs*—huge American chicken legs processed and frozen in plastic, sold cheap from the U.S. as aid relief, because Americans prefer white meat. When Edik balks at their size I say, "We've got radioactive chickens," and get a smile.

My American summer clothes are useless, so I've cobbled together an all-Russian wardrobe, which means uncomfortable pleather shoes and tight polyester sweaters in ghastly colors not found in nature. Short skirts, thick tights that bunch up at the ankles, and a broken-zippered coat that's thin as a blanket. And even in this, people stare at me and know: I'm an imposter.

In the subway stations veterans, gypsies, and amputees have started planting themselves in the corridors to beg, clogging the already jammed traffic flow as people struggle not to step on them. Some reek of urine and alcohol; others have signs explaining their plight; others are cleanly dressed, with their uniforms on and their medals displayed on velvet pads as proof that they should not be penniless. The Russian word for them, *bomzhi,* comes from *our* word, bums. Like everyone else Edik walks past them with alarm and shame, and once they're out of earshot he says to me, "I guess you're used to this, but we never had this before." They've all heard all about our hordes of homeless people.

Crime has arrived too, both petty and semiorganized. I still feel safer than in the U.S., but everyone here talks of pickpockets and street punks and mafiosos who demand payment from every kiosk owner or else burn the kiosks to the ground. They smolder along the sidewalks in the mornings.

What I do is throw parties. It's the most unembarrassing way to feed people. I say, "Bring your friends, anybody you want," and I load up the table and put on some music and they eat and fill the room with Russian words, and they teach me things like how not to piss off shop clerks. Tonight I've made grilled cheese sandwiches, deviled eggs, and fried potatoes. There are pickled vegetables, vodka and dollar-a-bottle champagne, *vafli* cookies and those awful little round *bubliki.* The custom here, at least right now, is not that the food goes together in any particular way, but that you fill the table, empty the cupboards, offer up everything you can find. I'm OK with that. I'm earning more money than I can manage to spend here. The stack of dollars on the top shelf of my armoire keeps growing as the ruble collapses and the supply lines for products seize up.

Tonight they're asking about supply and demand, because I said something offhanded like, "The more rubles they print, the less they'll be worth," and a few of them looked at me like this was gibberish. Maybe I said it wrong.

"But a ruble's a ruble," says a girl at the end of the table.

She's not an idiot, not completely naïve; she just hasn't been taught, year in and year out, that greed is the only reliable rule on the planet. I hesitate. Do I want to be the person who teaches her that? But the lesson is already breaking out in the streets.

Edik changes the subject for me. "I read somewhere that in America you can tell what kind of person someone is by the type of car he drives." Everyone laughs—it's absurd—but then the relative truth of that rumor dawns on me. There are lots of things I can't tell them about my country—things that embarrass me, things I don't understand.

When the party's over Edik sticks around and does what I'm told few Russian men do, the dishes. When I try to throw away some stale bread, he stops me and says that's a sin. When everything's cleaned up, we lean out the windows by the balcony so he can smoke, and I watch his lips kissing the black air, watch his bulbous Adam's apple bobbing in his throat. "What's the word for that, again?" I say, putting my fingers on it and feeling the hard ridges of his windpipe. I've taped vocabulary lists to the walls, and Edik just smiles and points at one of them. *Kadyk.*

To keep the cockroaches at bay I collect up the garbage and take it out to the stairwell, opening the creaking trash chute as quietly as possible. The walls are thin and I try to sneak around unnoticed.

But tonight I fail. My next-door neighbor unlatches his door with a fury and swings out. "You mustn't throw those away!" he hisses.

I stare at the old man, terrified, holding my plastic bag like it's a bomb.

"The bottles," he says. "The bottles," though I know the plastic bags are at least as valuable. He shuffles over and takes them.

Although I give money to almost all the beggars I pass, I haven't yet given to him. This is because when I walk by him on the sidewalk—kneeling in his army uniform, with his rows of medals—he ducks his head or turns away, pretending not to see me, not to live next door to me. And I don't want to steal this last illusion from him.

МАЯКОВСКАЯ

In the newsroom at the wire service I work the evening shift, and they pay me in dollars, not rubles. They hand us printouts of short articles, and we translate them into English as fast as possible, like machines. We learn all about the fighting in the Caucasus and the declarations of independence everywhere and the rise of new government officials in each former republic. When I meet up with terms I don't know, which is often, I ask the guy next to me, who's endlessly patient. Tall and thin, a Russian Mr. Rogers, he speaks English with such hard, curling, American R's that everyone presumes he must have been a spy at some point. When we ask him, he just shrugs and says, "Well."

Every hour or two we go out on the balcony for a smoke, where we gossip and look across the square at the huge lit-up statue of Mayakovsky, who looks as suave as a male model, with one hand pushing his suit coat back at the hip. Only Russians could make a poet look this powerful and sexy.

There's such an excess of news to sell to the West that we can hardly keep up, so they bring on a new translator from Boston who just spent the past three months in Tbilisi, trying to scrap together a documentary about the civil war breaking out there. "It's the most beautiful place in the world," he says. "They have wine." But when he and his crew broke their equipment and ran out of money, they came to Moscow to regroup. All kinds of makeshift explorers are touching down here; some call it the new Wild West—all resources, no laws. After work the new guy invites me to a party he's going to. When you meet someone from your own country and they're not an immediate asshole, you are friends.

I consider calling Edik to meet us, but the lure of speaking nothing but English for a whole night is too strong.

The apartment containing the party is a shock: no wallpaper, no gaudy lamps, no chintzy laminated entertainment center filled with china and lace. Just a plain off-white room with a futon and a stereo, some chairs. People move freely about, sip from their drinks whenever they want, no crazy toasts. No shots. It's like going to Sweden for a night, or Finland at least. People don't even take off their shoes at the door. There's a handful of Americans and Canadians; a sleek, loud Italian woman; a German with slicked-back hair; a few Australians. Everyone in English, loud and fast. On the stereo it's Sonic Youth, then some weird French rap, then Blondie. I'm transported.

Around ten a big blond American powers through the door. He says, "Youguysyouwillneverbelievewhatjusthappenedtome."

In the snow outside, his taxi slid ever so slowly toward an old woman obliviously crossing the street. He and the driver started screaming, they bashed the horn, but of course it was broken. "By the time we hit her we must've been going just a couple miles an hour, but the buildup was horrible. This poor stooped lady. I thought we were going to kill her."

His cheeks are pink and alcoholic, the sides of his neck lightly pickled in the manner of someone who had a good dermatologist as a teen. His yellow hair stands up in stiff tufts, his eyes are raw blue.

"Well?" someone says.

"She popped up and started banging on the hood, demanding we pay her something." His face flashes between astonished and jubilant.

"What'd you do?"

"The cabbie started screaming at her, calling her a fraud. It was fucking horrible. I was like, hey, she's a babushka. I wanted to take her to the hospital, but she just got this zloi look on her face and kept saying, twenty bucks, twenty bucks."

Later I learn they're all in on a running dare: who can catch the most unconventional gypsy cab. Apparently, in times of grave civic collapse, when no one knows exactly who's in charge, you can flag down and get a ride from such things as a garbage truck, even a snowplow. The German by the window holds the record with an off-duty city bus. "It's true," the others vouch. I've been burrowing through the city by subway all these months; who knew?

I sit studying them from a corner of the futon. Part of me is revolted, but there's another part, the groupless part. The language coming out of their mouths is perfect and swift and takes no effort to follow. They have normal food like potato chips and beer. I saw bananas and a box of Frosted Flakes in the kitchen.

Last month, Edik and I were riding home on a train from a friend's dacha, and the little bundled-up girl across the aisle fell asleep curled in her grandma's lap. Touching. All of us lulled together by the bounce and clatter of the rails. Except all I could think was that *this* was his iconic memory of childhood travel, while mine took place in the back of a station wagon, locked in a private nuclear family, in a car unlike any he'd seen or would see. Memories so different they could never be fused. He reached for my hand, maybe sensing that I'd stopped breathing. It was nothing I could explain to him.

Eventually the guy who hit the old lady bumbles drunkenly toward me and flops down. "You're new." His name is Jacob. From Miami. Really? Miami.

He's saying, just to me, "We should have gone after her. She was limping, you know? This is gonna dog me the rest of my life." He's looking at his lap, where his hands are twisting the hell out of his shirttails. Only after he's done talking does he glance up, as if surprised to find me still here, listening. His eyes go all grateful as he takes me in, until something startles him and he laughs. "Wait, what is this you're wearing? You've got sequins, even?"

In the winter like this, when the light lasts only six hours a day, and Christmas is coming and you're just twenty-one, this kind of talk can seduce you. For the first time you understand why the word *language* so often comes from the word *tongue.* Of course it's this base, writhing thing you survive on, this thing that unfurls from your core, where you can't see its origins. You can try to escape yourself, but you're still here.

М БАРРИКАДНАЯ

Jacob has bath salts. A long, deep tub in a big, tiled bathroom with ceilings fifteen feet high. The place has been partially renovated for foreigners but retains the mysterious Soviet design trend of a transom window between the bathroom and the kitchen, so while I soak he calls to me from the stove, asking if I want pesto or red sauce. He wanders in and refills my wineglass, then leaves again. It's that kind of life now, all through the spring. He has satellite TV; he buys cases of wine; he wears a grown-up overcoat, though he's not yet twenty-five. We're on the twelfth floor of the famous Kudrinskaya Ploshchad building, one of the seven glories Stalin built to embellish the city's horizon. Everyone says the apartments are bugged, but we're not sure who would be listening at this point. The place is smoky and not very clean, but there are big windows framing the city, and a piano, and french doors between the rooms. For work Jacob does some kind of trading for an American firm—iron and steel, I think—but he seems to work little, and more for amusement than money. He dresses in suits that were clearly once beautiful but are now dingy and loose, with a spot somewhere on every shirt. He keeps his face angled down most of the time, glancing up to make eye contact only in nervous rushes.

He has an international phone line and lets me call my parents and friends. I expect thrilled, heartfelt conversations each time, but in reality our topics in common have dwindled. My friends from school are all on the verge of graduating, looking for jobs. My old roommate's engaged and says, "Why are you talking that way? You sound Canadian or something."

Like Jacob and his friends I no longer fit there, but I don't quite fit here, which would almost make us all fit together if we weren't just misfits by nature. These are people who speak four or five languages, who drift from one country to another every year or two, who keep dog-eared *How to Learn Welsh* or Turkish textbooks on the floor next to their toilets. Jacob can sit for hours just reading a dictionary.

With them I see another side of the city, the expat bars and hard-currency shops, where big guards check passports to keep out Russians because the only kind who would spend this sort of money would have to be mafia men or hookers—more trouble than they're worth. I see inside all the grand hotels—the breathtaking art nouveau Metropol, the French bakery inside the Cosmos, the Spanish restaurant in the lobby of the Moskva, where one day we wind up next to former senator Gary Hart, who broke my spirit freshman year with his campaign scandals.

We roam and roam. I have to jog every few steps to keep up as Jacob lopes absentmindedly through the city, chain smoking and occasionally stopping to point at a business and say, "Was this here last week?" I never know, but he'll stop a stranger to ask, chat for ten minutes with any willing Russian about the history of a neighborhood. When our cabbies get lost he gives instructions so detailed they double take him suspiciously.

Today we're down by the river embankment, in front of a sleek new Italian clothes store on a brand-new, deserted street.

"We should go get you something nonpolyester."

"Hey, I'm fine. Do you know how fast this stuff dries?" I'm still doing all my laundry by hand, in my bathtub.

He draws me inside anyway, and the clerks greet him as if they know him already, but maybe they've been trained to do that. He makes odd humming sounds to himself as he picks his way through the store. Hovering over a stack of women's sweaters, he says, "This color would be good on you."

To see merchandise displayed for us to fondle, instead of trapped behind counters guarded by babushkas, gives me an anxious giddiness, and I can tell that the shopkeepers, though trained to accept the practice, still rise up on the balls of their feet as they watch us making ourselves at home.

I shake my head and twist away as he holds up a sweater to me. It's soft as a rabbit, pale blue-gray, and simple, probably dry clean only.

"You're never going to blend in anyway," he says, gesturing at my Russian ensemble. "Not like this, anyway." He says to the shopgirl, "Guess where she's from."

She's model beautiful and blushes, shakes her head. "Davaite," he says. Come on.

She shrugs and smiles helplessly. "U.S.A."

I make a swift move for the door and lean against the wall outside, mortified for some reason.

He saunters out and lights a fresh cigarette and reaches back for my hand as he starts to cross the street. I put my hands in my pockets and watch him go.

He glances back just once, then heads through a vast construction zone toward the river. The truth is I'm all turned around, I'm lost, and there's not a car or metro station in sight, not even a bus stop. What have I been doing? It's a gray, drizzly day and the light is fading and his hulked-over figure is getting smaller and smaller. When I'm close enough that he can hear my footsteps he slows down and waits for me, stretches back a hand for me to take. At the far edge of the construction we have to climb a low fence to get to an old red wooden tugboat on the river that seems like something out of a *Popeye* cartoon. Onboard, there's a beautiful mahogany bar inside, and we are the only foreigners. Again, the bartender says hello as if he knows Jacob, and when I respond in Russian he smiles at me as if I'm a charming accessory. We sit in a small booth by a window, and the water outside brings me back to the vast, brown Mississippi.

"So north is that way?" I point upriver, desperate to reclaim my bearings. "Does it run north and south?" Jacob laughs and pulls a battered map out of his coat, and I'm faced with the maze-like path of the river through the city. "It goes just about everywhere. It's no kind of landmark to use. How can you not know this?"

I tell him to quiz me on any part of the metro map, but he just shakes his head. "That's easy. That's tourist stuff." He orders us some Dutch beer and then sets a bag on the table. It sits there, tissue paper and all, through three rounds.

"You should try it on at least," he says once we're managing smiles again.

The bartender's drunk and glancing over conspiratorially. I peel off my glittery green and pink turtleneck and shiver in my dingy t-shirt for a second while Jacob bites the tags off the sweater and hands it over. He tilts his head to one side to take me in.

"Well?"

A slow smile spreads across his face. "What are you so afraid of?"

I shrug. "Nothing." But it comes out like a bluff.

Suddenly Jacob straightens his posture. A lanky blonde is headed right toward us. She's Russian; it's obvious from every sleek move. He stubs out his cigarette but doesn't stand up, and she surveys me with the briefest of glances as he introduces us.

"That was fun the other night," she says in Russian and starts to prattle about a dance club they apparently went to last week. She places one long slender hand on his shoulder, and he holds still. It's hard not to be intimidated by the seemingly flawless Russian women who hover around foreign men, acting as though they'd do just about anything to get a ticket out of here. They're gorgeous and smart and perfectly fluent—walking, breathing language coaches operating on their own turf. Jacob sighs and avoids looking at me. I focus on the water out the window.

"Oh, come on," he says outside afterward. "You have Edik."

"Right," I say, but of course I don't. Edik's not an idiot, and I couldn't lie to him. I haven't seen him in months. I haven't fed anyone, haven't thrown any parties. I take the metro home alone in the sweater, and sit on my balcony through half the night, trying to remember who I used to be.

M КИЕВСКАЯ

I've missed the deadline to start school in the fall so I stay another two months, socking away money for tuition. By Christmas I'll be home, or where home used to be. Sometimes I go for walks with Anna Petrovna but mostly I leave my apartment just for work and food. When I get especially lonely I go down to a little pizza place that's opened up not too far from work and I sit at the bar and order two beers and one pizza margherita. They have CNN on satellite, and all the lonesome new expats with no friends and no Russian skills sit around staring at it.

One night they show a clip of Bill Clinton playing his saxophone on Arsenio, and it makes me blush. Then somebody plops down next to me, saying, "Nu, privet," in a deep, familiar voice.

It's Andrei. He has a big bruise across a third of his face and a scab through the middle of his left brow.

"What happened to you?"

He shrugs it off. "Car accident," he says, but that feels like a lie.

"How's business?" I say.

"Outstanding. Bez problem. Better all the time." He owns four kiosks now, and is looking into buying a bar.

"Good for you. And you don't have . . . opponents?" I say, wondering about his face.

He shrugs. "Everybody has enemies. That's just business."

A soccer game comes on and we talk about that for a while. We share a pizza and a couple of beers, no shots, no toasts.

"Oh, I'm going to be a dad," he says. "In March."

"Wow," I say, in English, because he always liked the way that sounded.

"*Owow,*" he says, in a slow and careful effort.

"You should really call Edik, before you go," he says at the end of the night, and I nod. I know I should, but where would it land me? I give Andrei my parents' address and phone number, just in case, for the future. A few weeks later, I'll translate an article about a Russian businessman killed in a drive-by shooting on the steps out in front of this restaurant. It won't be Andrei or Edik, but for a minute my brain'll go white with the possibility. There'll be more of these kinds of shootings to come, many more.

The last night I remember of the city is election night, 1992. Some American companies sponsor a party at the Radisson Slavyanskaya Hotel, by Kiev Station. They put out an open invitation to Americans to come watch the returns all through the night into morning. Some people from work talk me into going, and I'm both drawn and repelled by the prospect of seeing Jacob there. It's been weeks. Over a thousand people show up, more Americans than I ever imagined were here. It feels like a huge high school dance, except we're of all ages in our motley jeans and wet boots, with our limp hair and tired eyes as the night goes on.

There are free Nestle Toll House cookies and Pop Secret popcorn and Coke, free Pizza Hut pizza and Miller Lite and KFC. They've got big screens set up all over the room, projecting the returns on CNN, and when the chairs fill up we lounge across the floor—unthinkable behavior in the city around us.

I spot a cluster of Jacob's friends by the Miller Lite stand, and they wave me over so I walk the plank. It turns out he's moved on to Prague for a new job, and I won't run into him here or anywhere again. "Prague," they say, capturing a whole room of jealousy in one word.

Ross Perot splits the conservative vote and this chubby sax player closes the gap. Carol Moseley-Braun becomes the first black woman senator, and a cheer goes up in the room like I've never heard. I realize, shouting and clapping, that I'm being louder right now than I've been in all eighteen months here. I've been sneaking around, keeping my head low, for so long. And no matter what anyone says tomorrow, tonight we're bound by something tinged with pride. Never mind that Moseley-Braun will get mired in corruption and Clinton will become a national embarrassment—like drunk, dancing Yeltsin, who's been selling all the nation's resources to five or six men. We don't know that yet. We drink and dance and try to believe, for now. Around dawn I drag my bones downstairs and out the front door, where I watch two women getting into an official black taxi outside, right in front of the lobby where they cost triple. They're laughing and stumbling like college girls, so young. I zip up and walk down the street a few blocks to hail a normal car for a dollar, and the driver asks me what the heck I've been doing all night. The sun is starting to come up. I tell him about the election, about the whole ridiculous party, free food and everything. He says, "Yeah, but how do you know Bush will really step down? Why should he yield to this new guy?"

Despite everything I've learned here, the question still strikes me as ludicrous. "He just will," I say. "That's how it works."

"But what if he doesn't," the driver says. "He probably likes being president, after all."

"He just will," I say, looking out the window at the cold river curving beside us, cutting its crazy route through the vast city. All these months I intended to memorize its path, but I never quite got around to it, and in the end I never will.

IT WAS THE screaming that woke Nick up—actually, the realization that the screaming was coming from him. His hands, he noticed next, were bleeding, were banged up. The hood of his car was a rupture of metal. He had to lean to one side to get a full view of the minivan in front of him. An accident, an accident. Before he could get a grip on any of this, a chain of boy scouts came filtering out of the van, pointing their thrilled little fingers at him. His fault.

Then he must have slipped under again for a second, because next thing he knew people were knocking at his window, and he could see their lips making all the motions of concerned language. He rolled down.

They were police officers—so quick—asking him if he was all right, if he knew what had happened. He nodded.

From the looks of the pavement, they said, Nick hadn't even

touched his brakes. It was midmorning, a hot, hazy weekday, and there were no drinking binges or faulty equipment to blame.

"Well." He looked from the cops to the minivan mother and back. "I guess I blacked out a little."

The minivan mother lost none of her fury, but the cops grew a lot more compassionate. The trouble was, this resulted in an ambulance. And no amount of protesting after that point could get Nick off the hook. He was carted away like a specimen, and through the back windows of the ambulance he could see a tall, hairy man hooking his car up to a tow truck. He was caught.

At the hospital everyone was waiting for him to black out again so they could watch. They did blood tests and eye tests, an EEG and a head CT. They checked his reflexes and his urine and blood, then after a lot of consulting resorted to alien, sci-fi phrases. *Transient ischemia. Petit mal. Tonic-clonic. Simple-partial.* He got the sense that every time they left the room they were hustling back to some reference library to locate in big leather books all the phrases they had failed to memorize in medical school. The orderlies shuttled him from room to room, floor to floor, and each new person he met required a fresh explanation of his circumstances.

"Let's try this again, for my sake," the latest doctor said, taking out his penlight. He was much older than all the rest, with veiny cheeks and big ten-year-old glasses that magnified his eyes.

Nick pulled the icepack away from the bump on his forehead and allowed this doctor, too, to lift his eyelids one at a time and scan his pupils. He blinked away the flashes until he could see the room again. "It's like a hiccup, a little skip," he mumbled.

"How long has it been going on?"

Nick shifted his weight, ripping the paper under his legs. "Two, three months?" he said, because this was what he had told the other doctors. Who knew if it was true? It was hard to fix a starting date.

"Do you notice the spells lasting longer, getting worse?"

The episodes had been so minor at first, Nick had thought maybe he was imagining them. Maybe they happened to everyone. "You know how when you're driving along with the stereo going, and you hit a bump in the road and the CD skips ahead just a beat?"

The doctor stared at him so uncomprehendingly that Nick wondered if maybe he'd switched off again and missed some new development in the conversation. He waited for the doctor to say something or react. But he didn't.

"It's like that, only everything around me skips—traffic, road signs, the clouds—everything jerks ahead just a little. You follow me?" Nick was the regional sales rep for three restaurant franchises, and spent twenty-five or thirty hours a week in his car. It was his central frame of reference, and they had towed it away with all his features inside.

"I lose time," Nick said.

"What you're describing may be a kind of seizure." The doctor worked up a serious expression.

"*May* be." Nick pulled his shirt tight across his thumping chest. "May be."

"I'd like to keep you here for observation." Nick pictured himself on an institution bed, a bunch of white coats with clipboards eyeing him all through the night.

He said no. He buttoned up his shirt and concentrated on his tie—*over, around, under*—letting the doctor's words slip through the air around him. *Abnormal electrical activity. Absence spells. Possibility of stroke, atherosclerosis. Tumor. Cyst. Mass.* He pictured a clump of Silly Putty left under his skull like a prank.

"Well, which is it, Doc?" Nick said at last. "Just tell me which one it is."

The doctor folded his arms and proposed more tests. Nick saw flashes of horror film images: himself on a metal table, head shaved, with red lines on his scalp marking future incisions.

"You're being childish," the doctor said. What did he know?

"Listen." Nick made a move for the door. He was sweating. "I appreciate your concern. I assure you, I swear, if it happens even one more time I will definitely go in for a second opinion."

The receptionists confronted Nick with a series of papers to sign, then pointed over to the corner, where they said his emergency contact was waiting.

"Emergency contact?" Nick said. And there she was, Theresa Felangi, stooped over in a long, loose skirt, studying the fish in the waiting room's aquarium.

"This is embarrassing," Nick said.

"Not at all." She smiled. Her hair was a different color, more reddish, and the freckles he'd always liked on her cheeks had multiplied. Three years ago they had nearly moved in together. Nick had terminated his lease and given away his old college couch, his posters, his porn, but at the last minute Theresa had a change of heart. She'd had a powerful dream about her future, she told him, but then she stopped talking and only shrugged. Apparently the dream hadn't featured him.

And now she was probably married, all settled, and Nick hadn't even gotten around to replacing her name on his insurance forms.

He followed her through the revolving doors, apologizing for the mix-up.

"No, it's good to see you," she said as they reached the curb. The afternoon had arrived, muggy and high pressure, leaning toward a summer storm.

When Nick offered to take a cab she looked offended. "You're not well. I'm driving you home."

He just wanted to get back to his car. He thought of the paperwork, the spare shirts, the phone, the travel mug.

"Shouldn't you just leave your things for now and go home and rest?" she said.

"It's not that serious."

"It sounds kind of serious."

For a second Nick had a woozy sensation of falling, but he didn't fall, didn't even teeter. "The thing is"—he put on his salesman voice—"there are better specialists over at Rockford Memorial. I'm going to make some appointments over there tomorrow rather than waste time here."

He snuck a look at her to gauge her expression.

"OK," she said. "OK." She turned onto East State Street, heading toward the impound lot.

After that they didn't talk for a while. As Nick watched the gray cars and buildings roll past, a brief fantasy imposed itself: They were forty years older, gray haired, and round shouldered. She drove everywhere because his sight was failing. They were going to McDonald's for coffee. Theresa wore thick stockings that sagged at the ankles and he wore a sweatshirt with a stain at the top of the belly. Then the jolt of a pothole snapped him out of his dream, and they were thirty-one years old again and separate, trying not to look at each other. "Are you still making those art projects?" he mustered.

"Not the action figures," Theresa said. When he had known her, Theresa had been teaching graphic design classes at the community college and in her spare time making little wax action figures in various female forms and professions—executioner, meter maid, guerilla princess—which she sold in the summers at art fairs, without much success. "I'm doing collages now," she said. "But they don't sell as well."

He nodded. He never knew what you were supposed to say about art. "Still living over by the water park?" Big raindrops started smacking the windshield with a kind of random violence.

"No," she said. "I've got a house on the west side, off Auburn. And a dog."

"And a husband?"

"Holy shit," she said. They had pulled into the impound lot and she'd spotted his car. "Wow, look at it."

Nick got out and walked over to his car. He crouched next to the left front quarter panel and ran his hand along the warped and jagged wheel well. "Well, hell," he muttered.

"I'm sure it's fine," he said, turning to Theresa. "I can drive it to the shop."

She leaned against the car parked beside his. "Nick, you can't drive."

He wished she would stop looking at him this way.

"I mean, you're *hurt*." She reached her hand out to his forehead.

"I'm fine." Nick shrugged her off, hearing the anger steeping in his voice. "This isn't some big dramatic thing, Theresa. It's a bump on the head. A fender bender."

"If you're blacking out, the police will probably revoke your license or something, make you get tested."

"Can they do that?"

"They should." She'd outgrown the old timidness, he saw, and acquired that confidence of women who didn't need anyone new in their lives. Nick imagined a snug little house for her, a dog and a husband and some flowerpots out front.

"You know, Theresa? I guess you don't really get to decide this one for me."

She stared at him for a while. "Right, fine. I'll tell the women and children to get off the streets then. And give me a head start, would you?"

Nick smiled back grimly. He could handle it. He watched her hustle into her car and drive off.

He crouched down again and pressed his palms against the cool metal of the dented hood. It seemed important to check on the basic facts. The episodes had started to make him wonder if the world in front of his eyes was the same one he saw inside his head. But the car was still here, still definitely mangled.

He thought of rust, of old age, of the impossibility of life without driving. He got in and buckled up.

"All right," he said to himself, turning up the stereo. "Now concentrate."

Concentrating didn't matter; it happened again on the drive home. Waiting at State and Alpine for the light to change he watched a can collector pushing his shopping cart slowly along the sidewalk. Nick watched the man's trench coat flap and billow in the wind at the back of his knees, and he felt sorry, for a second, as the man stooped to shield himself from the rain. And then he was gone. One blink—though Nick wasn't even sure he *had* blinked—and the man was out of sight. Not gone, as it turned out, just thirty feet farther along, and heading into a gas station, still stepping slowly. It was as though a hundred frames had been cut out of the film Nick was watching, or the cruel bastard above was screening Nick's life, pressing FAST FORWARD and SKIP just for the fun of it, out of boredom. The light had turned green, the cars had moved ahead around him. A few were backed up behind him, honking. Nick pulled over and put on his hazard lights. It scared him. What if he blinked and never woke up? He regretted sending Theresa away. But he couldn't sit there all evening. He left his hazards on and crept along in the right lane, giving himself a wide berth.

....

At home, his neighbor Bryan was working in the garage when he pulled in. Their building was a strange arrangement: a small warehouse built in the sixties, with the first floor converted now to one massive garage, and the upstairs done up in two big, mirror-image apartments. Although technically they shared the garage, in reality it was mostly Bryan's domain. He was a welder for a tent and awning company, but what he really loved was vehicles. He had two snowmobiles, a jet ski, a souped-up Corvette, and a giant pickup truck. There were extra sets of tires and tools hanging on all the walls in neat rows, and big glossy red tool cases standing below them. He even put in an old couch and chair, and when the weather was good he would open the garage doors and sit down there with a beer, watching the sun set across the Whitman Street Bridge. All Nick needed was a corner to park his car in, so it was a good setup all in all, low rent because the neighborhood was industrial and deserted, and Bryan was a nice guy, could fix anything. Sometimes Nick would sit upstairs on his couch at night feeling the low rumble of Bryan's machines in the garage below, or imagine him sitting on his own couch next door, facing Nick like a mirror on the other side of the wall.

"What the hell happened?" Bryan slapped his car lightly when he had parked and gotten out. He was tall and thin, a few years younger than Nick.

"Fender bender."

"You OK?" Bryan pointed at the bump.

"Yeah."

"This where your head hit?" Bryan pointed his torque wrench at the center of the crack in the windshield.

Nick nodded. "I guess so. Or my hand maybe." He ran his fingers over his forehead.

"Concussion?"

Nick shook his head. "Just a little one."

A few years back Bryan had been in a terrible accident; an old man pulled out in front of him on a country road. It shattered his knee, cracked his femur, and sent his girlfriend flying out the windshield and skidding twenty feet down the road. She had to have plastic surgery. But they each got a hundred grand from the insurance company. Bryan bought his Corvette, and his girlfriend left him for Florida.

Nick realized then that they weren't alone in the garage. In the ratty armchair near the staircase, in the shadow of a big arc welder, sat a girl with shiny red hair, cut short. She was maybe eighteen or nineteen.

"Hi." She waved when Nick finally noticed her.

"That's my sister. Bridgette."

"Bridge," she said. She was holding a bottle of pinkish wine.

Nick introduced himself. From across the room he could see that her face was cluttered with piercings. They flickered in the light when she turned her head. She was barefoot, in a stretched-out t-shirt and skirt. With her legs curled into her chest, her whole body fit easily into the chair.

"I didn't even know Bryan had a sister," Nick said to the room at large.

"Yeah, I keep her a secret."

"I've been living out west," Bridge said.

As Nick passed her on the way to the staircase he noticed a series of short whitish lines marking her calves. They were scars, all lined up and identical. She stared up at him with heavily made-up eyes that had been turned an unnatural bright green with contacts.

"Take this to Mike's on Twentieth Street," Bryan said, slapping the car again.

As if she had noticed and wanted to enhance Nick's discomfort, Bridge opened her mouth, dark and pink, then flickered her tongue stud at him, so briefly he thought he must have imagined it.

In his apartment the answering machine was picking up a call. On instinct he hustled over to it, but then stood there, trying to think of how he would explain himself. How could he say to his boss, his friends, his clients, I've got *abnormal electrical activity* in my brain?

The caller hung up without saying anything. He put some ice in a towel and took the phone over to the couch and lay down. He turned on the TV and flipped through the channels, settling on a Bulls-Lakers game.

The phone rang again, and he stared at it. Maybe it was the doctors, he thought suddenly. Maybe some test had come back explaining everything, showing how it was temporary, fixable—a vitamin deficiency, stress. Something psychological. He picked up the phone.

It was Theresa. "I only wanted to know if you made it home OK. That's all."

"I'm here," he said. "I'm fine."

"OK," she said, and the line went silent. "Well, OK. Good."

An image of her hands confronted him. She had stubby, nail-bitten hands that were always ink-stained, riddled with hang-nails. And when she talked they wrestled around through the air, improvising their own sign language. He didn't want her to hang up. He said, "I'm sorry I was so rude before."

"I'm sure it was a hard day."

On TV Kobe Bryant made a three-point shot and drew the foul. "You never answered my question, before."

"No, I didn't," she said.

"Well?"

"What was the question again?"

"Have you been to that new restaurant by the river?" he said.

And then there was the beeping sound of a call long dead. "Shit." He looked at the phone in his hand. He'd slipped away, gotten lost, and right in front of her. He called her back, and her phone rang four times, five times, six. Not even voice mail.

"Idiot." The ice had melted some and was dripping down the side of his head onto the couch cushions. He set the mess down on the coffee table and probed the bump with his fingers. He wished the skin were broken. If it could bleed a little, he thought, the bump might go down and be invisible by morning. He had a sales pitch in Peoria tomorrow. Of course it wasn't that kind of bump, though. It was firm, solid; no amount of bloodletting would delete it.

Nick went into the bathroom to inspect it. Though the bump was the result, not the cause of his blackout, he felt like placing the blame there. It was still numb from the ice, but when he pushed down hard enough he could tell it was tender and bruised. He pressed again, this time with the heel of his hand to spread the pain across his forehead.

"Yup." Across the knuckles of his right hand another bruise was blooming, where he figured he must have smacked the windshield or the dashboard.

The painkillers weren't in the bathroom so he started searching the cabinets, but in the middle of this the lights flickered and failed. It was dark.

His heart surged; his back started sweating. This was it, he was going under again.

He could hear every last little sound on the block. Traffic and rain and heartbeat commingled. The A/C unit started making dripping noises. Wait. He was here, awake. It wasn't his head, but the power. A power outage.

He groped his way down the stairs to the garage. Bryan and Bridge had pulled the couch and chair over by the garage doors and were sitting near the opening, just out of the rain, watching the storm evolve.

"God's telling us to take a break," Bryan said.

"There's lightning." Bridge patted the couch cushion next to her. "Have a seat."

Nick slouched into the sofa reluctantly and tried not to stare at her. She had a series of silver hoops threaded through the side of her right eyebrow. There must have been six or seven of them. A thick silver bullring hung from between her nostrils. "Have you guys got any painkillers, by chance?" he said.

Bryan handed Nick a beer from the twelve-pack on the floor, and Bridge rifled through her bag, boasting about her resourcefulness. She pulled out a passport, a ruler, a toothbrush, a switchblade—she had all the essentials of life in there. She shook the bag up and down near her ear, listening.

"Aha." With a flourish she pulled out two bottles—Tylenol and Advil.

Nick pointed at the Tylenol.

"How many?"

Nick didn't know. "Two?"

"I usually go for three," she said. "It's quite a bump." She stretched her hand out to his head slowly, as if preparing to pet a mean cat. Nick leaned away.

"OK."

"Actually . . ." She pulled out another small bottle and waved it at him. "These are some kind of homeopathic remedy thing." Nick decided to stick with the Tylenol.

The sky cracked open in a flash, and they all ducked their heads to see more of the storm through the garage doors.

"Getting closer," Bryan said.

"Maybe we should order a pizza," Bridge said.

Nick felt one of the pills stuck in his throat and swallowed hard against it. "I'm in."

By ten o'clock they'd run out of beer and the storm had passed, but the power hadn't come on. Nick went up to his apartment with a flashlight and found a bottle of Scotch a client had given him. He flashed the light at his answering machine, wondering if Theresa had called back, what she was thinking of him, if anything. But of course the machine was dead. Nick imagined her over in a little house with her dog, alone with her collages in the dark. He dialed her number again; she had called him first, after all. That was something. And maybe this whole episode today, the mixup with the hospital contacting her, maybe it was fate. Maybe, as people said, things happened for a reason. But she didn't answer.

Back downstairs, Bryan said, "I hate that stuff," when he saw the Scotch.

"Me too." Nick poured three glasses anyway. He had felt pretty good since the Tylenol and the beer, and was almost entirely adapted to Bridge's piercings, though he still had trouble keeping his eyes from the scars. She had them on her triceps too. They were having a good time though, the three of them, and Nick hadn't had a single episode, as far as he could tell. Maybe the faulty circuits of his brain weren't getting worse. Maybe he'd just had an exceptionally bad day and tomorrow his life would do the right thing and ease on back toward normal.

"I wish we could go to a movie," Bridge said.

"Too late," Bryan said.

"I know. You should get a home theater."

"Yeah," Bryan said idly, as if he just hadn't found the time yet.

Bridge told them about her friend Moon in Portland who had spent two years in a state forest, as a park ranger, with no TV, hardly any radio, just trees and trees. "She came out of it totally changed," Bridge said. "A revelation, you know? First thing she did was buy a home theater with all the money she'd saved." Bridge went on for a while, telling them how this Moon had decided to apply to film school and devote her life to making nature documentaries that people could watch instead of going camping. "Think about it," Bridge said. She spoke with a slight lisp from the stud in her tongue. "It's ecotourism squared. Nobody even has to ruffle the leaves. You send in a couple small camera crews, and everybody can just stay home, camp out on the living room floor with these videos in. No bugs. No littering. No spoiling the animals' habitat."

She leaned back proudly, to let Moon's dream sink in.

"That's the stupidest thing I've ever heard," Bryan said.

"Shut up. This could be the wave of the future."

"Virtual camping," Bryan said. "Right."

"What do you think?" She nudged Nick's leg.

"I don't know." Nick didn't like to take sides. "I guess anything's possible."

"See?" she said to Bryan.

He ignored her. He was slouched so thoroughly in the armchair that only his head was still vertical and his Scotch glass balanced easily on his stomach.

The rain had stopped but the pavement outside still shined wet in the streetlights. Occasionally a truck or an old car would drive by, the mist hissing up behind it.

"So that's why I had to leave town," Bridge said.

Nick blinked at her, then at Bryan, who was dozing soundly, his Scotch glass resting safely on the floor beside him. It had happened again. What had he missed?

"Pardon?" Nick said.

"You're such a space case. I'm not going to repeat the whole thing."

"I'm sorry." He touched his forehead again. He didn't know where the ice pack had gone.

"Are you OK?" She reached over. "Are you feeling all right? You don't look very good."

"Really?" He scrutinized her expression.

"Really. Do you want more painkillers?"

He took a few more pills from her.

"So what's your problem?" she said without accusation. Her voice was low and calm. The rain started up again with a light patter, and they both stared into it. "Are you always like this?"

He turned to face her. It was darker inside now, but he could still make out her features and the thin white lines along her calves. "What happened here?" he touched one finger lightly to the skin above her ankle.

"Scars," she said. "Don't you have any?"

Nick thought about his body for a minute. "On my knee. And my right hip. From a dirt bike accident."

"Anywhere else?"

He pushed up his sleeve and showed her the back of his forearm, which was criss-crossed with thick, jagged scars. "Put my arm through a window once, by accident."

"Wow." She leaned in for a closer look. "That must have bled."

A semi roared past down Madison Street, leaving a cloud of mist in its wake. "What about you?" Nick said.

"Oh, me, yeah. I have that problem," she said. "Cutting, you know, all the rage."

"Cutting?"

"You know. It's in the news and everything." She made a quick slicing motion across her forearm, then rolled her eyes. "Totally stupid, of course."

He was trying to swallow but couldn't. "Do you still do it?"

Bridge sighed and glanced over at Bryan, who was still dead asleep. "When I was born," she said, "I didn't have a single birthmark. Can you imagine? What would they do, I used to think, if they lost me? How would they ever identify my body?"

"Is that why you do it?"

"I don't *do it* anymore." She was getting restless. "And no."

"Why, then?"

She stirred her finger through her Scotch. She had hardly drunk any of it. She looked at it, then put the glass on the cement floor with a clink.

Nick felt like one of those doctors, so clinical, so aloof. "I have this problem," he said. "I lose time."

Bridge's face flashed to life in an excited smile.

"That's how the accident happened today." He gestured toward his mangled car. "I'll be going along like a regular person, and then, poof." He snapped his fingers, this time without much energy. "It's like the world has jumped ahead of me by a couple minutes." He saw himself, for a second, as a tiny man balancing like a logroller on a miniature planet that spun and spun and sometimes bumped him off.

Bridge's eyes were wide like she couldn't believe her luck.

"Do you know what I mean?"

"Sure," she said. She held up both hands like a film director envisioning a scene. "Like a crack in the facade."

Nick waited for her to explain.

"It's like, you know. *We* live out here, outside your head, and you live in there, inside. And sometimes the two get out of sync." She matched her hands up palm to palm, then shifted one sharply to the side. "It's like *The Matrix.*"

He suppressed a laugh. "Well. Maybe."

"What do you see in those lost seconds?" she asked.

This hadn't ever occurred to him, and now he wondered about it, searched his memory, but came up blank. "I don't see anything."

"Oh." She nodded smugly, as if she were an expert on this now. "Maybe you're not trying hard enough."

"I'm trying to make it not happen at all."

"Why?" she said. "Maybe they want to show you something."

He opened his mouth, trying not to smile, then closed it again. "*Who?*"

"Well, I don't know who. *They,*" she said. "Whoever it is you believe in."

He shrugged and sighed. "I don't believe in anything like that. I believe in *this* world." He leaned down and tapped the cold floor with his knuckles, reviving the bruises there.

"Oh," she said, disappointed.

They sat in silence for a while, until he couldn't take it. "What?" he said. "You think I'm being stupid?"

"No. No, I don't. You're being perfectly normal."

"But I'm not normal."

"Right," she said. "You have this problem."

He could hear the disdain creeping into her voice, and he thought to himself, *she's nineteen, what could she possibly know, go to bed.* He imagined Theresa coming over to visit, letting herself in and slipping into his sheets until he awoke to the faint smell of her red wine breath, her Carmex. Her curly mass of hair would fill the pillow beside his head, and if she woke up in the night, he would be there, rapt. He would not fall asleep on her.

"You have a problem too, you know," he said.

"Why?" She recoiled. "What? Because I . . . *modify* myself? Look at indigenous tribes and stuff. People have been doing it for ages."

"Not that." Nick gestured at her face. "*This.*" He reached out and placed one hand on those ridges of thin scars along her calf. He felt them, really felt them. It was like a topographical map brought to life under his palm.

She smiled as if she held the secrets of the universe somewhere back in her throat, and *wouldn't he like to know.*

"You might be interested to know," she said, "it brings a certain clarity, the cutting."

Just then the scene jerked ahead for Nick, but only by a second or so. Still, he could feel it, like the woozy rush of waking up with the sensation that you're falling. And the glass that had been in his hands was now a mess of shards on the floor. He gripped his knees and tried to settle his breathing.

"It just happened?" Bridge said.

He nodded. "What did it look like?"

She only shrugged. "It wasn't so long," she said at last. "Don't worry."

"You were talking about clarity?"

"Right. Like this." She plucked a hair from his head. Nick flinched and scratched at it.

"Were you awake just then?"

He was. He could see it now, silly as it must be, but he could see it all unfolding before his eyes. Like when he would cry over a scrape as a kid, and his dad would swing his fist overhead, joking, *I'll give you something to cry about.*

"Does it hurt?" he asked.

She shrugged.

He turned his head from side to side, trying to shake the idea away. "What on earth is the matter with you? With us?"

Bridge laughed. "Nothing. This is just living."

He felt revolted and sad and captivated all at once. The light was glinting off her bright, dyed hair and bouncing from metal to metal along the contours of her face. Was she the future or the past, a vision or just the flattest, basest reality? Had she come down to save him or pin him to the ground? He didn't care. He felt the blood sizzling through his capillaries like the spray of the cars outside, and he wanted to see it, to pry apart the shell of his skin and see what he was made of. Still, he was afraid to look directly at her, so he stared ahead into the dark, empty street, and reached across the couch for her hand. He said, "Show me."

SEPARATE KINGDOMS

"You'll be ok for an hour?" Colt's wife, Cheri, leans over him, breasts safed away in that monstrous cotton jogging bra. Her Lycra-skinned legs are green with white racing stripes. Tae-bo. She's going to the basement to kick herself silly.

He'll be fine. He's reclined on the scratchy couch in the back room—the old couch, in the reject room—convalescing. Hank, their sheltie mutt, stands up at the end

When I get home from school he's still back there in the reject room. Five days and counting he's been living there, in his habitat. Whenever he lets out Hank and Eddie he goes outside and pees with them. He leans against the Grangers' fence with his pajama bottoms pushed down in front and tilts his head to the sky, for the whole entire neighborhood to see.

The kids on our street told the kids on the bus, and

of the couch, eyeing Cheri in anticipation.

"You're not going anywhere, Stench," she says to the dog. She strokes Colt's stubble one last time and walks out.

She's sucking up to him, feeling sorry. The dogs aren't, and he respects them for it.

He balances the remote control against his thigh with the heel of one bandaged hand and carefully, without moving his fingers too much, gets himself to *Animal Planet.* They say before long he'll have full range of motion in all the remaining fingers, but for now they're thick and sluggish with trauma, anxious for any wrong move.

Eddie, the McGradys' other dog, a twelve-year-old liver-colored shorthair, lumbers in from the kitchen and stands between Colt and the TV, scanning the couch for an the kids on the bus passed it all around school, so today in marching band it went like this: Alex Schoper started staggering around with his fists in his armpits, scratching and making monkey noises, then pushing down at his crotch. "Wooh wooh wooh." He leaned up against me and Jason and Sadie, pretending to pee on all of us.

"Your dad's really losing it, Slap-Jack," he said, as if that was some revelation. He waved his hands around, thumbs tucked in, till he got a good laugh out of everyone.

It would've been smarter of me to just walk away. But no. I guess I don't come from smart people after all.

No sense thinking about it anyway. There are helpless scientists trapped in the House of Doom, and so far I've rescued two from the zombies. 69,250 points. I've open space. "Mrrrrrl," he says. "Mrrrrrl?"

"Oh, all right. Whiner." Colt lifts his legs up off the couch. "Well, come on." With his jaw he gestures toward the area under his knees, and Eddie climbs up warily, because the rules about furniture fluctuate. The dogs settle in donut shapes side by side, and Colt sets his legs gently down on their backs. Eddie stares up at him for a few minutes and then closes his eyes, content.

It's six o'clock and *Water Warrior*'s on. He hates Mike Teak, the show's British host, who approaches the animals like an inquisitor. But Colt harbors a vicious belief that one day the animals will win, one day the sharks or alligators will bite off Mike's arms and legs, leave him screaming, "Oh, look at that!" in his queeny accent, and Colt blasted the venom-spewing Bat-Zombie but there are still the biting spiders and all the little bats.

"Jack, why don't you take a break and keep your dad company while I exercise?"

As if he wants company. From me. As if he's said a complete sentence this week at all, to me or her or anyone.

The zombies come at me from all sides. I shoot and shoot. Their limbs fly off, arm, hand, foot, but they keep on coming.

"Hey, killer." Mom palms the top of my head and tilts my face upward, and I die. "You alright? You OK?"

I don't tell her about band practice, and she doesn't seem to notice the red part of my cheek that's all numb and tingly.

"OK, OK," I say. "I'm doing it." I put down the controller and go through the kitchen doesn't want to miss that episode.

"Bull sharks have a sharp eye for food," says the female *Water Warrior* assistant, who may or may not be Mrs. Mike Teak. They have a strange intimacy. "And when they're hungry, they size up anything that moves as a potential meal."

"Dad?"

Jack stands skinny in the doorway, just twelve, and spooked too, by the hands.

"Mom says I'm supposed to come and sit with you."

Jack is a boy with imagination but he doesn't understand about the animals, those bumbling, lost-in-the-suburbs moose, or the baby tiger sharks using their fins to walk across the sand. Jack doesn't understand the envy that swells in Colt every time he watches them.

"Do I have to?"

to the back room, which smells like a mixture of hamster and hospital. There he is, under his afghan, my dad. The one everybody's talking about.

His hands are hard to look at, hard to think about. I lean on the door frame for a long time, waiting for him to notice me.

"Dad?"

The way he stiffens up it's clear I'm the wrong sight, saying the wrong words again.

"Mom says I'm supposed to come and sit with you."

He turns back to the TV, where it's another animal show, of course. I swear he'd like to stick his hand through the screen, grab one of those exotic trees, and pull himself right through to the jungle, the river, the ocean. Leave me and Mom behind to fend for ourselves.

"Do I have to?"

Colt shakes his head no, and Jack goes back to the living room, to the God Almighty Xbox.

"This is how a crocodile will catch a bird in the wild." Mike Teak is back after a commercial. It's a new location, and he's leaning over a pier, holding a duck-sized bird by its feet over the water. The bird flaps its wings and squawks as a crocodile thrusts itself high out of the water, searching at the air with its open mouth. On shore, some onlookers ahhh and screech, and the croc's jaws snap shut in a flurry of feathers. But Mike Teak has pulled the bird away just in time. It's alive but maimed, and the croc sinks into the water unsatisfied. "We ask our animals to work for their food, because it's a natural way for them to behave."

"Asshole," Colt says to the TV. He grabs for the remote,

He shrugs me off, and now he'll sit in there sulking, and it'll be me who was the bad guy. I mean, Jason Beasley's dad plays House of Doom with him. When you go over to Jason's house, it's like Mr. Beasley knows your name and your high scores and everything.

Maybe that's a little pathetic I guess. Mr. Beasley's laid off all the time anyway, no wonder. Not my dad. For him it's always been nothing but work—night shifts and overtime, then moping around half asleep by the TV, looking like he wished he was dead. Nine years he sweats away in that dump hole at the hydraulic press. And then smash, one wrong move, and they send you home like this. Parts of you gone.

I'll never get to go to college. He'll never get all the things that all that work was supposed to buy.

forgetting to be careful, and is startled back to reality by the strange pain there, under the bandages, where his thumbs aren't anymore.

"It's not much comfort," Father Henry said in the hospital when Colt woke up after the accident. "But try to focus on the things you still have. You have a lot to be grateful for." Right, grateful.

"In time you'll adapt," Father Henry said, and he meant well; he wasn't a tool. He even stood there and let Colt seethe at him, just absorbing it. "You'll learn how to do everything you did before."

Sure, everything. Colt had nodded dimly. He was sedated with horror and pain meds. One minute it was 4:30 a.m. in the machine shop and he and Mauricio were on a coffee-and-ephedrine buzz trying to stamp out one last batch

From the top of the basement stairs I can hear my mom down there doing exercise. She's shouting along all cheery with that creepy Tae-Bo guy, calling out all the punches. Fine, she keeps saying whenever anyone asks. We're fine. As if she isn't sneaking back to their bedroom once a day so he won't catch her crying. We're all just perfectly normal, if you ask her about it. But his thumbs are gone. Clean off, never coming back. We aren't fine. Even Alex Schoper knows better than that.

I go back to the living room and start up the game again. The scientists come out of the mansion, three of them. They're hysterical, waving their arms and crying, and inside there are seven or eight more, innocents. They need me.

I reload my gun and approach the house. The porch

of tractor wheel covers before shift's end. They'd opened the computer boards on the punch presses and bypassed the interlock to speed things up—which was against policy, sure, but how else could they finish on time? And the next minute—well, there were those minutes in between. He didn't remember them in the hospital yet, but they'd been coming back to him in fits and flashes since. All he knew in the hospital was that they'd been making very good time with those wheel covers that night, in and out, in and out, stacking them up for shipping. And then the next minute Father Henry and Cheri were hovering over him, telling him he was going to be just fine.

You try it, Colt wishes he'd said to Father Henry. *You* light a cigarette, zip your fly, grab a beer. Beat off. Can you do it?

The doorbell is ringing. boards are rotted, and if you step in the wrong spot you can stir up swarms of biting spiders. Or fall through to the basement, where the zombies feed and breed and play cards. It's practically certain death. But I get past the bad spots and kick my way through the front door. Here they come, arms groping and shaggy. I fire, fire, fire.

Somebody's at the door, staring at me through the little window. Not in the game, in our house.

It's Harris, the guy who owns the machine shop. He came by yesterday but my dad wouldn't let us answer the door.

"Sweet Christ." I ignore him, hoping he'll go away before my dad catches sight of him.

"If you ring that doorbell," I'd like to say, "you're going to be sorry."

Naturally, he rings it.

Eddie and Hank blink and struggle out from under Colt's legs. Over the TV and the Xbox and the basement DVD strains of Billy Blanks and his karate-chopping women, you can hear it: You can hear them not giving anybody ten minutes of peace in their own goddamn home. It rings again, and Hank will not stop yelping. Colt pokes one finger awkwardly at the volume button.

"I was wondering why he's so skinny." Mike Teak is knee-deep in some river now, black night all around him, and his canoe bangs with a hollow sound against the rocks. He's holding a little croc, two feet long. It writhes and squawks in his hands like a baby pterodactyl. "But you can see what's happened to him. He's had part of his jaw broken off. And actually it's gone. You're missing part of your jaw, buddy! Quite de-

Hank comes racing in, starts his battle cries, and Eddie follows behind, howling. "Shut up," I say, but they're disobedient little beasts.

"Mom?" I yell toward the basement.

It rings again. "Mom?" I go to the top of the basement stairs. "Am I supposed to answer it or not?"

She comes huffing up in a second, wiping her face, which is shiny and red and almost healthy looking. "I'll handle it, Jack. Why don't you go downstairs and practice?"

When she opens the door I go hide in the kitchen, on the far side of the fridge behind the rabbit's cage.

On Monday a lawyer came by, the second one I think. He said not to talk to Harris or anyone. He said he'd see that we got justice, which sounds good and all, but come on. Have a look around.

bilitating. But he's been able to get enough feed. He's fat enough. You all right, mate, you all right?"

It's his boss, Harris, at the door. Colt can hear him in there, talking up his own wife in his own living room, with his own son looking on. He sinks lower into the couch, draws the afghan up.

"Eddie?" he says. "Eddie, get in here!"

Hank won't listen, it's useless to try. But wise old Eddie comes back. He's conflicted. He stands by the couch and longs for the living room.

"Sit." Eddie groans and shifts his weight, touches his haunches to the floor for a second, then stands up again. "Disobedient little beast."

Cheri's good at getting rid of the visitors, sometimes without even letting them in the door. But she's plagued by courtesy, this woman. And after the guy left, the fighting from the back room was epic. She was calling him unreasonable. He was calling her a gold digger, her of all people.

I get it, how the money won't fix anything. But it might be enough to move out of this house, to a different bus route, maybe even a different school. A whole different town.

"I don't hear you practicing, Jack," Mom yells toward the kitchen.

I can hardly hear them anyway. So I go downstairs and pull the string for the light bulb and sit down at my drum kit. The knuckles across my fists are red and bruisy. My first real junior high fight, not little kid flailing but knock-down-drag-out. It would have been great except for that miserable section at the end where I had to run off before anyone could see how much it shook me.

Harris, well, he owns half the shit in town. Harris gets what he wants.

"He's just so conked out, you know," Cheri's saying, trying to send him off. But then there's a rustling in the hall, and fat, gray Harris steps right into the reject room. A bottle of Jack and a box of chocolates in his hands—which still work fine.

He puts his presents on top of the TV and looks for a safe place to sit. Everybody else usually sits on the floor, but Harris plucks a few things off the cat's chair and sits down right in it, not advisable. He rubs at his bad knees and unzips his red XXL windbreaker.

It makes you not even want to be in band.

My drums, at least, are the best in school: a red Pearl five-piece that Dad and me bought off some creep down on Seventh Street with track marks in his arms. The guy sat down to play for a second, like he wanted to show off for us, but it was just painful. He was like a grown-up future version of Alex Schoper, banging away like a caveman, without any control of the rudiments whatsoever. Whenever I sit down to practice I think of guys like that, and how I don't want to be them. So I start up my single-stroke roll, real slow and even: Duh. Guh. Duh. Guh. Duh. Guh. Duh.

Guh Duh Guh Duh Guh Duh Guh Duh Guh Duh Guh Duh
Guh Duh Guh Guh Duh Guh Duh Guh Duh Guh Duh Guh

"Here we go," Colt groans, and Eddie shudders. Jack's at the drums again. Two hours a day, every day, without fail.

Duh Guh Duh Guh Duh Guh
Duh Guh Duh Guh Duh Guh
Duh Guh Duh Guh Duh Guh
Duh Guh Duh Guh Duh Guh

The boy's obsession is everybody else's misery.

"The lawyers told me not to come here," Harris speaks up, throwing a magnanimous smile across the room. "'Course they want to handle this their way, get their cut."

"I was saying how tired you've been," Cheri says from the doorway, looking like a bear caught in her den, fuming but for the moment just tracking the scent and gauging the angles. "How the pain medication makes you sleepy. And you're supposed to rest."

Harris says, "The way I see it, no reason two grown-ass men can't work this out themselves. Am I right?"

Cheri perches on the edge of the couch, mostly blocking Colt's view of Harris, which is a fat relief. Sweat shimmies down her neck, and the veins there duck and pulse like dark worms in good soil.

Duh Guh Duh Guh Duh Guh
duh guh duh guh duh guh
duh guh duh guh duh guh
duh guh duh guh duh guh
duh guh duh guh duh guh
duh guh duh guh duh guh
duh guh duh guh duh guh
duh guh duh guh duh guh
duh guh duh guh duh guh
duh guh duh guh duh guh
duh guh duh guh duh guh
duh guh duh guh duh guh
duh guh duh guh duh guh
duh guh duh guh duh guh
duh guh duh guh duh guh
duh guh duh guh duh guh
duh guh duh guh duh guh
duh guh duh guh duh guh
duh guh duh guh duh guh
duh guh duh guh duh guh
duh guh duh guh duh guh
duh guh duh guh duh guh
duh guh duh guh duh guh
duh guh duh guh duh guh
duh guh duh guh duh guh
duh guh duh guh duh guh
duh guh duh guh duh guh
duh guh duh guh duh guh

"We're not making any decisions in this condition," she says.

Harris smiles and nods like she's the most reasonable woman in the world. Then he shifts over to catch Colt's line of sight again.

"Maybe you and I should talk this over in private, you know. Might be things about this situation not everyone would understand. Work things," he adds, glancing back to Cheri.

It's a kind of dare these types enjoy making: *Can you not control your wife, in your own house, on your own filthy goddamn couch?*

"Give us five minutes, Babe," Colt says, holding her gaze for a while, wishing they had some secret code.

She exhales; she gets it. It's a debt he'll have to repay later. But she leaves.

Harris calls little Hank

duh guh duh guh duh guh
duh guh duh guh duh guh
duh guh duh guh duh guh
duh guh duh guh duh guh
duh guh duh guh duh guh
duh guh duh guh duh guh
duh guh duh guh duh guh
duh guh duh guh duh guh
duh guh duh guh duh guh
duh guh duh guh duh guh
duh guh duh guh duh guh
duh guh duh guh duh guh
duh guh duh guh duh guh
duh guh duh guh duh guh
duh guh duh guh duh guh
duh guh duh guh duh guh
duh guh duh guh duh guh
duh guh duh guh duh guh
duh guh duh guh duh guh
duh guh duh guh duh guh
duh guh duh guh duh guh
duh guh duh guh duh guh
duh guh duh guh duh guh
duh guh duh guh duh guh
duh guh duh guh duh guh
duh guh duh guh duh guh
duh guh duh guh duh guh
duh guh duh guh duh guh

over to his ankles and starts petting him. The dog's going to pay later too. A long time seems to pass. On TV a commercial for Canada comes on, big open vistas and mountains, people who look like their problems are solved. Finally Harris coughs and says, "We both know what happened in there that night."

"That so?"

Harris opens the bottle of Jack and offers it to Colt. Colt holds up his bandaged hands. "You gonna hold it right up to my lips?"

Harris looks away, takes a swig, and regroups. "We both know, like everybody else in that shop, my *employees*, it isn't even possible to have this kind of catastrophe with those machines by accident. That's a fact any six-year-old kid could prove."

It's the truth, but what difference does the truth make

duh guh duh guh duh guh
duh guh duh guh duh guh
duh guh duh guh duh guh
duh guh duh guh duh guh
duh guh duh guh duh guh
duh guh duh guh duh guh
duh guh duh guh duh guh
duh guh duh guh duh guh
duh guh duh guh duh guh
duh guh duh guh duh guh
duh guh duh guh duh guh
duh guh duh guh duh guh
duh guh duh guh duh guh
duh guh duh guh duh guh
duh guh duh guh duh guh
duh guh duh guh duh guh
duh guh duh guh duh guh
duh guh duh guh duh guh
duh guh duh guh duh guh
duh guh duh guh duh guh
duh guh duh guh duh guh
duh guh duh guh duh guh
duh guh duh guh duh guh
duh guh duh guh duh guh
duh guh duh guh duh guh
duh guh duh guh duh guh
duh guh duh guh duh guh
duh guh duh guh duh guh

anymore? The credits are rolling on *Water Warrior* but another one comes on right after.

"Listen, I'm not here to make enemies. I'm here to work this out. *I* don't want to be in court for ten years. Do you? I don't want OSHA breathing down my neck, contracts drying up, my name in the news. You don't either."

"I wish you'd stop petting my dog."

"I'm just here to tell you my lawyer's gonna make you a one-time offer. Two hundred grand and we all walk away. I don't report you for whatever tinkering you did to the safety locks, I don't sue *you* for endangering everybody else there, and bringing this bullshit on us. And you walk away with your disability pay and a fat check. Buy yourself a boat, pay off your house, whatever."

duh guh duh guh duh guh
duh guh duh guh duh guh
duh guh duh guh duh guh
duh guh duh guh duh guh
duh guh duh guh duh guh
duh guh duh guh duh guh
duh guh duh guh duh guh
duh guh duh guh duh guh
duh guh duh guh duh guh
duh guh duh guh duh guh
duh guh duh guh duh guh
duh guh duh guh duh guh
duh guh duh guh duh guh
duh guh duh guh duh guh
duh guh duh guh duh guh
duh guh duh guh duh guh
duh guh duh guh duh guh
duh guh duh guh duh guh
duh guh duh guh duh guh
duh guh duh guh duh guh
duh guh duh guh duh guh
duh guh duh guh duh guh
duh guh duh guh duh guh
duh guh duh guh duh guh
duh guh duh guh duh guh
duh guh duh guh duh guh
duh guh duh guh duh guh
duh guh duh guh duh guh

"Who says I want your money?"

Harris looks down with a dry, tired-out laugh. One hand rises up, loses its purpose, and falls back to his thigh. "It's a damn mystery to me what you want."

"Light me a cigarette," Colt says, pushing the pack across the coffee table with his fingertips.

Harris fumbles his way through this little bitty task and then holds out the lit cigarette, floundering. Colt holds still and waits until finally the old guy gets up and steps over and sticks the thing right in his lips. A great nourishing inhale, a pleasure not lost yet.

This takes the juice out of Harris. He swigs again from the bottle, puts the cap on, pushes it away. His face is a billboard of regret about coming here.

"This is the best offer

duh guh Duh Guh Duh. Guh. Duh.

I like to do these for at least ten minutes, but before I'm even halfway I notice a strange thing moving around up by the window well. It's an arm waving and knocking against the window.

When I go over and climb on the table to look, it's Sadie, from band. She's a trombone. She's crouched down in the window well, with her braids falling in the dirt.

you're gonna see. It's downhill from here, I promise you."

"Duly noted." Colt melts himself into the couch, becoming part of the landscape.

When he sees Colt's not going to say anything else, Harris dusts himself off and heads out, seeming maybe a half-inch smaller. But he'll swell right back up in his car on the long ride home.

Cheri comes back in and sits at the foot of the couch. "He's a delight."

"I don't blame him."

A burst of air comes out of her mouth, seeming to spray her eyes open.

Colt would like to fold his hands behind his head, elbows in the air. Instead, he fumbles just to stamp out his cigarette. "He wants to settle. Two hundred grand."

She just keeps shaking her head. "No. We call back that lawyer, the first one, the nice

"You forgot your bag," she says when I open the window. And sure enough there's my stupid backpack, as if I needed another reminder of how I ran off like a loser, forgetting my drumsticks and everything.

She pushes my bag through the opening.

"I'm not supposed to have people over this week," I say.

"I'll be quiet," she says, wriggling herself through the little window and landing hands-first on the table next to me.

She jumps down and stands in the middle of our basement, looking around and blinking. Under the light bulb, all the little hairs that have rubbed out of her braids make a fuzzy halo.

"So this is your house."

"Just the basement."

"It's like ours." She nods. They're all pretty much the same around here.

one. If Harris wants to settle this fast he must know you'll win."

Colt rubs one fingertip against his eyelid and gets a whiff of his own rank, bandaged palm. "We'd be done with it. Right now. No hassles. Pay off the house and still have a chunk of money."

She slaps her thigh. "And then what? What exactly comes after that?"

He stares past her. Mike Teak paddles through the Coola Coola Swamp with his voluptuous female assistant, who doesn't have a British accent.

"Tell me, Colt, really. What's your plan after that? How long do you think $200,000 will last?"

But all he has to do is hold up his white-bound hands, and she goes all soft. "I just want to hear what's going on in your . . . in *you*."

"These your drums?" She goes over and runs her fingers along the cymbals, which, it's true, are not very quality. It'll be years before we can save up for better ones, I guess.

Now she's moving around behind my drums, looking at all the pictures taped to the cement wall, which no one has ever really done before. I get this weird feeling suddenly that she's poking around, that maybe she's come to get an up-close at my dad, like he's some kind of field trip exhibit.

But when I walk over it's clear she's just squinting hard at those pictures, which have nothing to do with my dad. They're just magazine cutouts of the greats—Charlie Watts and Keith Moon, John Bonham, Neil Peart. They mingle around behind me, cheering, whenever I sit down and play.

"I guess it's stupid," I say.

Colt shakes his head and closes his eyes.

Her long fingers come to rest on his thigh, and she moves them up and down, getting warmer. "*Why* wouldn't you want to make them pay?"

He won't answer.

"I know this is overwhelming. And it's going to take some time to get back to feeling normal, but—"

"I'm not going to *be* normal again." That was the whole point. He's determined, not bitter, about that.

"Exactly. So what kind of job—"

Colt sucks in a great pocket of air and releases: "Squaaaaaaaaawk!" The sound rifles through his throat and fills the room beautifully.

Her face contorts. "Pardon?"

He sighs, defeated, and peers out the dark window. "Digga Digga."

"No," she says. "This guy, look at him go." She's got her fingernail on a shot of Buddy Rich all hunched over and fierce, looking like he's about to take a bite out of his hi-hat.

"Apparently he was an asshole, but he was the best. If you're the best at something, you can get away with stuff."

She makes little sighing noises as she goes down the wall, putting her nose close to each picture. "It must be hard, the drums."

"I could show you."

Her eyes flash like it's too good to be true, so I hand her a couple of sticks and show her how to hold them. I let her sit at the snare and I reach in beside her and show her single strokes, double strokes, building up to a nine-stroke roll I do, which has accents in all sorts of weird spots to blow your mind.

"Wow," she starts to giggle

Now her teeth come out, yellowed and harmless. She's trying to make light. "OK. If you think this is fun for me . . ."

It's a blue-sky banner day in Coola Coola, and Mr. and Mrs. Teak have taken their dog, a friendly midsized black lab, along for the ride, and he trembles at the front of the boat, making himself small. He would make great crocodile bait, Mike notes, so they'll want to be very careful with him.

"Colt." She snaps her fingers. "You're not alone in this choice. This is my life too. And in case you've forgotten, there's Jack."

"A million dollars isn't going to fix this."

She stands up to leave but hesitates. "Three million, Colt, just in case you're interested. There's a case in Wisconsin last year that got 3.2 million."

when it's her turn. She pushes one stick at the snare, then the other, and I have to hold her wrists and jiggle them to show her how to be loose. What she's doing is a kind of a Dunk Dunk sound, heavy and ear-piercing and clinging to the skins. Erratic. It's the way most people start out. Duh. GUH. DUH. Guh. Guh. DUH. guh. duh. GUH. DUH. dugh. Guuugh.

She stops.

"That's all right," I say. I try to explain how much harder drumming is than it looks. People think it's just banging away like crazy. But really it's about precision and control, about dividing up the spaces between sounds into the tiniest, quickest little bits. Regular people can't even hear the difference. But they feel it. You get those sticks moving like hummingbirds, but it's not a runaway train, not random. It's all under control, all exactly

"You take it, then," he shouts, wishing he could throw something. "Take it! Take the goddamn money and the little drummer boy and drive yourselves straight to paradise. Set yourselves up!"

She comes at him with her hand out, pointing her finger at his face. "We're not going anywhere."

She snatches the remote off his belly, turns the TV off, and leaves, taking the remote with her.

The room turns an eerie greenish black, and he closes his eyes against it, but the images come back. Blood and machines and crunching metal. The sound of the alarms going off, Taylor and Mauricio leaning over him on the dirty cement floor when he comes to, wet screaming hands, shock, all of them shouting and bug-eyed.

And then he's in and out of it. There are masks and white jackets, an angelic,

the way you want it. You're the most perfectly tuned machine, dead-on, precise.

It's the shouting, from upstairs. It's my dad. My own dad. In front of Sadie and everything.

"It's different from trombone," I say.

She goes over to her backpack. I figure she's going to rush out of here, but instead she digs around in it and comes back holding out an iPod. "I stole it from my brother," she says. "There's some songs you might like."

She sits down on Mom's exercise mat and pats the space next to her. She holds out the headphones but I just can't move. So she lies back on the mat and puts the earbuds in, closes her eyes, starts tapping her fingers against her stomach. I can hear the beat brown-haired paramedic, rubber gloves, rubber gloves, needles and questions, and then stitches. In the end just stitches lined up angrily, and that strange pain, in vague flashes, where there is nothing but air.

They gave him ten days' worth of Vicodin, but he already took tonight's pill this afternoon. Maybe he should just take the morning pill now.

Nine years on the night shift and they expect him to sleep in the dark now. Just take a pill and sleep—close your eyes—like nothing could be easier. Close your eyes, close your eyes and stay awake, lamalamalamala. The sky is black out the back room windows. Shamalamadingdong. Shamaoomama. There is no world outside. A dark, empty space yawns open beyond the back door, and he's alone now, drifting in his ranch house through the luminous, hollow leaking out around her ears. I kneel down by her and watch.

She must feel that. She opens her eyes and smiles up, like I'm the only thing in the world. "Come here," she says, so I lie down next to her and she hands me one earbud so I have one ear and she has the other and the music rumbles through both our brains, mixing us together. It's an old Pixies song with a tight drumbeat, and in the background, over the lyrics and guitars, these strange voices start talking behind the song—a deep creepy man's voice and then some howling lady gibberish, and I think: *Yeah, her brother's got taste. Her too.* She puts the iPod on my chest and moves her hand to my rib cage, and it's like we're all one unit. A bunch of thoughts start tumbling through me, like for some reason there's Mrs. Kelly's voice, our health teacher, sky, tilting randomly spaceward with no up or down. And then the rooms of the house begin to break off and drift away, unburdening him, and his little room picks up speed. The stars, great fire balls, loom larger, then the walls and windows of his room shudder and are ripped from him in a freezing, galactic gust. His afghan billows up and sweeps away like a torn sail. The dogs are gone, the remote control taken, and he reaches for the couch cushions under him, until the writhing lights up the pain under his bandages, and he's jolted back to life.

Awake, he's released from it. The dogs are curled under his legs again, and Eddie groans. Colt pats him lightly on the head with his fingertips. "Close your eyes."

He tries to think good things, easy things. He thinks saying, *Your body's your kingdom*, over and over, and my mom saying, *You OK, killer?* And there's the hospital rooms and Alex Schoper and in the middle of all this something occurs to me but right then Sadie rolls in and kisses me.

"Wait. Hang on. Wait." I act like maybe I heard something upstairs. "Wait here."

I climb the stairs, and it's like I can hear my own blood pumping inside me. What occurred to me was a time a while back when my dad and I were watching *Whale Diaries.* It's a half hour a week of them sliding through the deep blue and making their creaking sounds. He turned away from the TV for a second, his face still moony, and said, "Look at all they have that we don't have." He said we thought we were in charge but all we had to show for it was shitty jobs, prisons, traffic jams. He said, of the shop, where he should be right now, standing around after break, finishing their cigarettes, feet barking, backs bucking. They head to their stations slowly, the coffee still hot on their breath.

It's not as bad as people think, much better than most jobs: no customers to please, no mindless chitchat, no dress code, and on the night shift, hardly any engineers or bosses anywhere. They're on their own. For the guys who have babies or loudmouths at home, it's easier, here in the grind of the machines, to keep their heads to themselves. In those dark, dead-of-night forgotten hours they become machines, all of them, their bodies on autopilot, their brains free to roam. Colt picks up a sheet of metal off the stacks, sets it in the press, fingers under, thumbs on top, and it comes to life in a hydraulic shiver and "You know what separates us from the animals?" And I said, "Our brains?" He held up his thumbs and wiggled them. "Opposable thumbs."

What occurred to me was, he crossed over to their side.

Up in the reject room it's so dark I can hardly see anything. The TV's off. I stand in the doorway, waiting for my eyes to adjust. His eyes are shut, his legs propped up on the dogs. He's kicked the afghan off so it's in a pile on the floor, with one corner of it still tucked under his butt. The first bandages were big boxing fists but these just wrap around his palms, not his fingers, and they make his hands look weird—longer and thinner than they really are. I wish they could have sewed them back on. Put the bones in the sockets, stitched the skin together. And then under the bandages would be his chug, its jaws bearing down, flash.

He's awake. He's sweating. He's home on the couch. It's dark. There are eyes on him. Sleep, he was sleeping. He was paralyzed with dream.

He drops back into it heavily, and is back in the shop moving his hands from the stacks to the press to the stacks to the press. His thumbs are intact and callused and strong. He looks from the left thumb to the right, and the press comes down again and again, as it's done all these years. In other dreams, on other nights, the machine has eaten him piece by piece, and he kept offering himself up to it, powerless as an addict. With each smack of the press now, Colt looks back at his thumbs, takes inventory, left and right, and he grabs another sheet of metal and feeds it thumbs, curled up and waiting to hatch fresh.

His body springs awake in a shock. I jump back. His eyes are huge, blinking at me: *Who are you? What have you done to me?* It's like he doesn't know whether to sleep or stay awake, but then, of course, he chooses sleep again.

And I think: *Dad.* I think: *Even now.*

I go back to the basement.

"It's OK," Sadie says. "You don't have to be embarrassed." She wants to lie down again. I just want to sleep.

The song has switched and now there are strange girls singing about monkeys in heaven and I try to pretend it's not really me here: It's some other kid with nothing in his head, just watching Sadie lean toward him again, and for a second it's like I'm passing out, moving out of the kingdom and into the air, which into the machine. Crack, still there. Smack, all ten of them. Colt counts the blows: sixteen, thirty-four, ninety-two, one-oh-eight, two-forty, and loses track and starts over. He stares into the green glow lights of the hydraulic press, that one-ton razor-edged monster, and he slips the metal nimbly in-out, in-out. His thoughts erode, go haywire in these long voodoo nights. As he gazes into the eyes of the machine he wonders, *Could he join it, could he be it?* In the vertigo of that crushing flash, he can't help but think, *What if?*

There are murmurs in his living room, strangers in his house.

"—hasn't talked yet to the OSHA officials?" says a man's voice in the other room.

"I don't know," Cheri says.

"Well, it's a little more complicated," the voice is say- is like getting free and lost all at once, a queasy feeling that makes me jump back from her.

"OK," she says. "Jeez, sorry."

Before I have the sense to fix it she's scrambling her things together and climbing back on the table by the window well, reaching up.

But she can't get out alone. The window's too high. She stands there, facing the wall, waiting for something.

"You don't have to go," I say.

"It's late."

"I liked those songs," I say.

She shrugs. "Are you going to help me climb out, or what?"

So I do. I get on the table and make a sling with my hands, like in gym class, and she steps in and scrambles up the wall, claws at the window frame, and I push her through.

"Hey," I say, hoping she'll turn around and say good-ing. It isn't Harris; it's that lawyer she liked. "If the safety mechanism was disengaged."

Stand a crew next to an express train track fifty hours a week, fifty weeks a year, and see what happens, Colt thinks. See how long it takes before somebody decides to step onto the rails.

"Disabling or obstructing safety features *is* an OSHA violation. So the question is, did Harris Machines bypass the safety lock, or did the workers do it?"

"You mean Colt, did Colt?"

They are finding him out, they are catching him.

"We can still win those cases. If we demonstrate that the employer placed unfair production expectations, an environment of pressure and risk—"

It's too much, all too much. Colt kicks away the afghan and upsets the dogs and bye or something, but she just keeps going, and I watch her ankles leave.

Upstairs they're shouting again.

I take my drumsticks and go sit at the top of the stairs, with my ear to the door. There's voices in there, which these days is not a good sign. I'd like to just go to bed now, but it's risky walking through there when they're going at it. You can get tangled up in it, hear things that rattle in your head all night.

I start doing a quiet little seven-stroke roll against my thigh: pa ter pa ter pa ter PAT pa ter pa ter pa ter PAT pa ter pa ter pa ter PAT pa ter pa ter pa ter PAT pater pater pater PAT pater pater pater Pat pater pater pater Pat pater pater pater Pat pater pater pater Pat pater pater pater Pat pater pater pater Pat pater pater pater Pat pater pater rushes through the kitchen to the front room. "Listen," he shouts. "We're not interested, OK? Do you get it?"

"Colt." The lawyer wastes no time with getting-to-know-yous. "It's natural for you to feel upset, but do you —"

"*Listen* to me in my home. I just want my disability. I don't want you nosing around, screwing up things with OSHA, bringing up all kinds of questions, OK?"

The lawyer just stays put, looking at Colt like he's a madman. Colt complies. He throws his arms up in a gorilla charge.

The guy backs toward the door, persisting, "We have a good shot here, no matter what you might've done. Or not done."

Colt kicks the door shut behind the guy and the noise vibrates through the house. Cheri's crying.

pater Pat pater pater pater Pat pater pater pater Pat pater pater pater Pat pater pater pater Pat pater pater pater Pat pater pater pater Pat pater pater pater Pat pater pater pater Pat pater pater pater Pat pater pater pater Pat pater pater pater Pat pater pater pater Pat pater pater pater Pat pater pater pater Pat pater pater pater Pat pater pater pater Pat pater pater pater Pat pater pater pater Pat pater pater pater Pat paterpaterpaterPat paterpaterpaterPat paterpaterpaterPat paterpaterpaterPat paterpaterpaterPat pater pater pater Pat pater pater pater Pat pater pater pater Pat pater pater pater Pat paterpaterpaterPat paterpaterpaterPat paterpaterpaterPat paterpaterpaterPat paterpaterpaterPat pater paterpaterpaterPat pater pater Pat pater pater pater Pat pater pater pater Pat pater

"What is going on?" she says. "What the hell is going on?"

Light-headed, Colt sits down on the couch across from her. He can smell the antiseptic on him and his own animal scent.

She has asked so little of him.

"What does he mean, tamper with the machine?" she says. "Why does everybody keep saying this?"

Colt wishes he'd taken the Vicodin, wishes he were asleep, obliterated, dropped off the edge of the planet so she could make a fresh start without him.

His hands, strange bundles, are throbbing on his knees. This is what he has left. "Two buttons," he says at last, and she stops whimpering and wipes her nose against her shoulder.

"Like here and here." He

pater pater Pat pater pater pater Pat pa ter pa ter pater PAT pa ter pa ter pa ter PAT pa ter pa ter pa ter PAT pa ter pa ter pa ter PAT pa ter pa ter pa ter PAT pa ter pa ter pa ter PAT pa ter pa ter pa ter PAT pa ter pa ter pa ter PAT pa ter pa ter pa ter PAT pa ter pa ter pa ter PAT pa ter pa ter pa ter PAT pa ter pa ter pa ter PAT pa ter pa ter pa ter PAT pa ter pa ter PAT.

gestures with both hands. "You put the sheet metal in and then you punch the buttons to bring the press down. One with each hand, so your fingers *can't* be in it." She nods vaguely. She doesn't follow, but she wants him to go on. She will never understand the steely lure of it.

"Cuts your time in half. And then it's just in out, in out, in out, you know, no buttons." He traces that gesture through the air, fluid, efficient, stamped into him. "And so . . ." He pauses. He's doing a pretty good job, he thinks. She's buying it.

"And so that's what we do some nights. That's what we all did."

She comes over to him slowly, puts her arms around his shoulders, crying, squeezing him, all of him, to her chest.

"I don't care," she says at last. "Honey, I don't care."

But it's not really any fun without the noise, and each stroke stings and throbs until that spot on my thigh is welted up under my jeans. I sit still and listen again, and they aren't shouting.

I think about us in a two-story house, someplace different. It wouldn't even have to be that nice. Just someplace by the woods with a big picture window, and no reject furniture, not even a reject room at all. He could sit in a nice chair and look out at the animals, and we wouldn't bother him too much, we'd just leave him alone. And maybe we could get him some high-powered binoculars for seeing things. And when Easter came we could take a vacation, maybe someplace wild like Colorado. We could be like those people who take pictures of themselves and hang them up on the walls.

He can feel the damp folds of her t-shirt against his cheek, can smell a little of her sweat, and for a minute he feels them go elsewhere together. They're drifting down the shallow Hidden River without Mike Teak or the camera crews, just the two of them. They lean out over the edge of the canoe and watch turtles paddle and walk, paddle and walk under clear, shallow water.

But there's a shift in the room, a presence, a noise from behind them.

"Dad?"

A jolt rips through him, way beyond measure or control.

"Jack, goddamnit," he shouts. "Would you quit sneaking around this house!"

"I live here," he says in his so-quiet way, and it's clear as the ocean just how broken he is, and who's to blame.

If he got that money we could do all those things, maybe more. It seems like such an easy plan to explain, and things sound so quiet up there. I don't know, but I decide to go on in.

In the front room she's holding him tight on the couch. His arms are around her too, the bundles of his hands resting behind her back, just hovering without touching, like it would hurt too much.

Maybe she's already broken through to him. Maybe the storm is over.

"Dad?"

He shocks up like I just Tasered him, and I screw it all up again.

"Jack, goddamnit," he shouts. "Would you quit sneaking around this house!"

"I live here."

His eyes are round and wild and I lose track of everything I wanted to say. Colo-

Jack holds his hands out with his fingers all spread. "I know why you did it. I think I understand."

Colt has to get out, it's too much. He brushes past Jack in a fury to get to the back room.

The kid was looking at him in a way that burned through the skin. And now he will know. For the rest of his life Jack will know.

The dogs dance and stomp behind him as he stands at the back door trying to work the handle. "Fuck," he says. "Fuck." At last he bursts into the night, leaving the door wide open, and he can breathe. It's late October and cold, so quiet. The skies are clear, bright stars overhead. Everything is right here just as he left it. He can smell carved pumpkins and burnt leaves, he can smell the chilled dirt all around him. Hank and Eddie set off to mark their things, rado, binoculars, are the only words left. I say, "I know why you did it. I think I understand."

Then he rushes at me. I duck against the wall, cover my head, and he sweeps past me like a tornado.

"Oh, Jack." I let Mom take a hold of me. I curl up on the floor against her legs. We're tangled together. Crying.

"What's happening to us?"

She shakes her head for a long time. "I don't know, honey."

Her face looks like something has died in it. She's emptied out and scared and she's not even trying to hide it.

As if she sees me noticing something I shouldn't see, she tucks her head back into my neck and rocks me for a long time. Then she says, "This money thing is your dad's choice. He's your dad, and he has his reasons. You know?"

and a train moans its way through the distance.

Colt steps up to the Grangers' fence and pushes down the front of his pajamas with both hands, then listens to the sound of his urine slapping the chain link and the ground in the stillness. That's better. Some fucking cold. When he's done, the dogs start barking, yapping, and Colt pulls the elastic waistband back up with two fingers and turns around.

The lawyer's standing near the edge of their property. The dogs are sniffing his legs.

"You got a beautiful family," the guy says.

"What's that supposed to mean?" Hank runs off after a tremble in the hedge, but Eddie comes to Colt's side.

"I just meant I'm sorry I upset you. I won't come back. You've got my number if you change your mind."

I say I do.

"It doesn't really matter," I say. "The money."

"That's right."

"Alex Schoper has money and he's still a total asshole."

"That's true of a lot of people," she says.

We're done rocking and crying, but she keeps holding me there, really tight.

"Yesterday I tried to do everything all day without my thumbs," I say.

She wipes her nose and pulls back to look at me.

"It didn't work at all." It's true. I never lasted more than a half hour at a time. Nothing worked right, and on instinct I kept grabbing stuff with my thumbs. Some things, like buttons, or the drums, were just impossible.

"I think that's very sweet, Jack." She pats my head. "I think you're a deeply good person. You know that?"

Colt regards him for a minute. "OK."

The lawyer smiles. "This one is gorgeous." He motions toward Eddie. "My grandfather used to breed shorthairs. Is he a hunter?"

The cold rustles through Colt's t-shirt and pajama bottoms.

"Eddie here couldn't find his own turd in a sandbox. Could you, Eddie?" He touches the soft fur on Eddie's brow with his fingertips. Eddie holds still and looks up, tail going. "Used to guard Jack's cradle like the Secret Service."

The guy laughs. "Yeah. Nothing like a good dog."

"You don't have one," Colt says. He can just tell.

He shakes his head.

Colt stares at him. He's a dark-suited machine.

"Well, I'll take off. I just wanted to apologize." He inhales deeply and starts walk-

I groan. That's not what I was talking about.

"Maybe we could try it together for a little while," she says.

It's been a long day. "The hard thing," I say, "is that you keep forgetting not to use them, and that ruins everything."

"I bet." She thinks that over. Her fingers are making circles and squares in my hair.

"But, you know, we could tape them up."

She stops with my hair. "That's a great idea."

So we go in the kitchen and find some masking tape in the drawer by the garbage can. We each tape our left hands by ourselves, putting the thumb across our palms diagonally toward our pinkies. And then she tapes my right hand, and finally together we get her right hand bandaged up. There's a lot of snickering.

ing away, then comes back. Of course he comes back.

"You'd be surprised how often it happens, Colt. You'd be surprised. Funny as it sounds, people even do it on purpose every once in a while. And it's not even unwinnable."

There are gears going around in this guy, pistons hammering, steam coming out his mouth.

"I guess you can't spend fifty hours a week in front of something that powerful and not have it affect you somehow." He pauses. Shrugs. "People are overworked."

Colt watches his jaws working up and down in the dark, with his hands poking out for emphasis at odd places. He thinks he understands, but he will never understand.

"There was a woman in Peoria," he's saying. "Worked at a—"

"Gaaah!" Colt shouts.

We smell like Band-Aids. My fingers are stiff and awkward.

"Well, what should we try?" she says.

"We should make cookies."

Her mouth opens up in a big smile and she laughs.

We do good teamwork but still everything takes twice as long. I drop the vanilla bottle and it breaks all over the floor. We have to hold each egg with both hands and kind of drop it on the edge of the bowl to break it, then fish out the shells. I try to hold the mixing spoon woven through my fingers, under over under, but once the flour's in, it gets too thick to stir this way.

She gets out the electric mixer and we have to use all four of our hands to keep the bowl and mixer in place. We're white with flour and sticky all over by the time they're cooked, and getting

The man blinks. Eddie barks. Hank comes trotting back.

"Worked at a lumberyard—"

"Zeeeeeeeeshandagahhh!" Colt screams, moving toward the man in monstrous, lumbering steps that shake the earth and rattle the trees and stir all the winged creatures.

"OK, good-bye," the guy says, hustling away. "Good-bye!"

The dogs join up and bark at him. Loyal, wise old Eddie starts chasing him, even though he knows it's only craziness. He chases the man all the way to his car, with Colt at his heels, barking along. Colt feels a little sorry for the man then and tries to form the strange consonants and vowels that might help the man understand.

"Aiim nahh," he cries into the darkness and then tries again one last time. "I'm not one of you!"

them out of the oven is scary. "Stand back." She holds her hands vertical to keep the mitts on and then pokes the tray around till she gets it in both hands.

But the cookies are good, ultra good. And she eats over a dozen. "God, I was so hungry," she says.

We lean on the counter with our elbows, side by side. Outside, it's a dark, cold night. The windows are black, and the house starts to shake as a train goes by on the tracks at the edge of the neighborhood.

"Well? Is it bedtime?" She pulls out the scissors and offers to free me. My hands are sticky and wet under the bandages, and they're starting to itch.

"I think . . ." I say after a minute. She waits.

"I think we should sleep this way."

About the author

About the book

Read on

Insights,
Interviews
& More . . .

There to Here

Jaci Sumner

IN THE 1980s there was a rumor in my hometown of Rockford, Illinois, that we were on the top ten list of cities the Soviets would nuke first, supposedly because of certain essential machine parts that we alone manufactured. Preposterous, I hope, but I believed it and concocted hundreds of ghastly nightmares about nuclear war and Soviet soldiers storming my house—ridiculous *Red Dawn* stuff.

Then in high school I had an economics teacher who pitched us all sorts of crude anticommunist propaganda praising the invisible hand of greed and portraying

Communists as obviously foolish and possibly downright evil. (In fact, I wouldn't be surprised if he were the one who started that rumor.) Suspicious, I decided once I got to college to take some Russian classes and see for myself. Officially I was an English major (and not a very good one), but gradually I accumulated a Russian major on the side. At the end of each semester I would say to myself, *Well, I still can't* speak *it, so I guess I'd better sign up for another round*. By my final year of college I still couldn't really speak Russian, which meant my only option was to go there.

I arrived in Moscow a few weeks after graduation, in June 1991, on the very day that Yeltsin was elected President of the Russian Federation—which didn't mean much, since Russia was still under the near-total control of the Soviet Union. But radical change was in the air, and by August of that year a coup toppled Gorbachev's regime and Yeltsin took over. Faster and less violently than anyone could have predicted, the Soviet Union disintegrated, poof, like a bad dream. And the republics it had once held together started spiraling toward bankruptcy and frightening political instability.

I found a job as a translator at a news agency, and for the first time in my life got paid to push words around a computer screen, which felt good. I had always wanted to write stories, but Moscow was the first place I started to feel like I might actually have stories to write. At the same time, I discovered how nearly impossible it is to tell stories with anything approaching accuracy. I saw how every newspaper in town produced a conflicting account of ▸

There to Here *(continued)*

the most simple and crucial historic developments, quoting sources who could almost never be trusted, and working in haste and invariably with incomplete knowledge. The very act of ordering something into a story removes the chaos and confusion of truth; stories make sense of things that in reality don't make sense. That's why we need them.

As an interloper in the strange chaos of Moscow, I was a misfit, but the position suited me. People at home couldn't fathom why I'd want to live in Russia, and people in Russia, though welcoming as could be, seemed baffled by my choice as well. All I knew was that I felt more alive occupying the precarious space between two worlds than I did being comfortably immersed in just one. It seems to me that the position of being alien, being an insignificant observer split between cultures, is a valuable one, and one that an astonishing percentage of writers occupy.

Still, it was several years before I actually started writing and finishing stories. By that point I was back in the states, in Ann Arbor, deep into a PhD program in Slavic literature that was snuffing out my will to live. I was too proud and frightened to quit, but I started taking fiction workshops at night to at least escape. I discovered that writing stories made me feel alive in the way that life abroad had; to do justice to a story I had to divide my loyalties between characters, never allying myself blindly with any one side.

And then something happened. My father suffered a ruptured aneurysm in his aorta, spent a month in a coma, and lost a leg from complications. It was one of those

“The very act of ordering something into a story removes the chaos and confusion of truth; stories make sense of things that in reality don't make sense. That's why we need them.”

life-rattling experiences that make you decide to quit wasting time and just do what matters most to you. So I quit. I switched to Michigan's MFA program. And the specters of disability, of alienation, of misfitting, started to haunt my stories. I wanted to write about the ways that things as inherent and inescapable as our language, our bodies, our families, can make us feel separate and out of place. And about the ways that bridges reconnecting us can rise up in unlikely places.

It's a big risk to attempt to capture cultures in your work that are not your own, to speak for or even about people whose experiences you haven't actually lived. But it seems to me that that is the job of fiction writers. There is only so much we can say about ourselves; sooner or later we have to jump beyond our own experience, and we may as well make a big leap as a small one. Stories are a way of building those bridges, too.

"I wanted to write about the ways that things as inherent and inescapable as our language, our bodies, our families, can make us feel separate and out of place."

Trivia

HERE ARE SOME miscellaneous notes about each story, and a soundtrack. For links to these songs and references, go to www.valerielaken.com.

"Before Long"

1. I believe the soundtrack for this story would be "Here Comes the Sun Again" by M. Ward (*Transistor Radio*).
2. I wish I could read stories within the time span of one song.
3. Though I love coming-of-age stories, I had always kind of wanted to write a story in which a kid comes to the precipice of adulthood and turns around and runs back. I think most of us actually do this a few times, stealing glimpses of what's to come before we work up the nerve to jump, or finally get pushed.
4. Not that there's much similarity, but I had Hemingway's Nick Adams stories on my mind when I was writing this.

"Spectators"

1. "What If" by Lucinda Williams (*West*).
2. In my mind this story is set at Lake Lawn Resort on Delavan Lake in Wisconsin, where my mother was once a lifeguard and my parents used to dance.
3. Legend has it that at the bottom of the lake there is a circus elephant who died during winter and, since it couldn't be buried in the frozen ground, was dragged out onto the ice and broke through during the spring thaw. Or something like that.
4. When my dad lost his left leg above the knee, his doctors warned it would be at least six months before he could even

be fitted with a prosthesis. We feared he wouldn't even want one, wouldn't even want to live. But within a few months he was walking with a flashy new C-Leg, and by six months he was competing in golf tournaments. And coming home with stories.

5. Even the briefest mention of amputation will grind most conversations to a nervous halt. I was interested in the ways that disabilities don't just affect people physically; they turn people into walking, breathing taboos. And we hardly hear their stories.

"Scavengers"

1. "For the Widows in Paradise, for the Fatherless in Ypsilanti" by Sufjan Stevens (*Greetings from Michigan*), although Califone's "Michigan Girls" (*Quicksand/Cradlesnakes*) is a close runner-up.
2. I wrote a wholly different version of this story many years ago, in my very first fiction workshop with Josh Henkin. Justifiably, nobody much liked it except me. Then last year I decided to write the whole thing over, using not a single sentence from the first version. It has only one incident in common with the first.
3. I'm a little obsessed with houses, with the roles they play in our lives. And when more and more homes and neighborhoods started going empty across America, I felt a pull to write something about it. Because Detroit had been suffering these kinds of losses for decades, and because I had lived near it for so long, it seemed like a good place to set the story.
4. Kevin Bauman's haunting photos of abandoned homes in Detroit were a big inspiration (100AbandonedHouses.com). I also recommend ForgottenDetroit.com.
5. Most of the houses in Bauman's photos look nothing like the ones in the neighborhood of this story. I wanted to capture one of the more ordinary working-class neighborhoods of small bungalows that have gone empty more recently and which can be purchased now for as little as $250.

"Family Planning"

1. "Pardon My Heart" by Neil Young (*Zuma*).
2. For a long time it seemed that every time I took a flight between Russia and the United States there was at least one couple with a small, distressed child they had just adopted.
3. On one flight I sat behind two women with a three-year-old Russian who kept asking her new mothers for juice: a simple, three-letter Russian word, *sok*. Neither of them had the slightest ▸

Trivia ***(continued)***

idea what she was saying to them. I leaned over the seat and translated. When we had pacified the girl and struck up a conversation, I wrote down the pronunciations of a few key Russian words for them: milk and water, juice and bread, and hungry. They gave the slip of paper a perfunctory glance and stuffed it in the pocket of their seat back, where they left it when they deplaned. Russian is a hard language; I have learned to concede this point. At the same time, this three-year-old child spoke it, their child. And her parents and grandparents, wherever they were, and everyone she had ever known. I couldn't stop thinking that within hours she might never hear Russian again. And within weeks or months she would forget it herself.

4. When I first met my Russian friend Nikolai, I asked what he did for a living and he said, "I sell babies." In reality he was an incredibly compassionate liaison for a very good adoption agency, but his discomfort with the transactive nature of his work stayed with me.
5. In a job interview once, a professor asked me to talk about the gender politics of this story, which made me consider climbing out the window. If it's about anything, and maybe it isn't, this story is about the politics of love, not gender.

"God of Fire"

1. "Dream" by Doug Martsch, from *Doug Martsch*—an album well worth buying if you somehow missed it.
2. Two masterful stories obsessed me while writing this story: Amy Hempel's "In the Cemetery Where Al Jolson is Buried" and Jamaica Kincaid's "My Mother."
3. Payne Stewart was a pro golfer with eleven PGA titles; on October 25, 1999, he was aboard a Learjet that apparently lost cabin pressure for reasons unknown. Both pilots and all four passengers went unconscious and at some point died, but the plane continued on auto-pilot, rising as high as 48,000 feet before the plane eventually ran out of fuel and crashed in South Dakota. All morning long CNN showed this mystery plane moving through the sky.

"Map of the City"

1. "The Summer" by Yo La Tengo (*Fakebook*). Really, the whole album.

2. But ideally the soundtrack for this story would be nothing but a Moscow subway train roaring between stations—each section punctuated by that woman's voice announcing the next station: *Осторожно, двери закрываются. Следующяя станция . . .*
3. In the summer of 1991, the exchange rate was around 27 rubles to the dollar, and if you handed clerks a 25 ruble note, they would gasp and gripe that they couldn't possibly break a note that big. By December 1991: 115 rubles to the dollar. By May 1993: 1,000 rubles to the dollar. By 1995: 4,500 rubles to the dollar.
4. When you ask people where they live in Moscow, there's a tendency for them to reply with the nearest metro station. I wanted to write a story shaped by the geography of the city, as mapped by the metro running under it.
5. The Moscow metro covers over 300 kilometers, with 182 stations (and growing), transporting an average of 7 million passengers per day. During rush hours, the wait between trains is only about 90 seconds.
6. As I was finishing this story, on the morning of March 29, 2010, two suicide bombers killed twenty-four people at the Lubyanka Metro Station and twelve people at the Park Kultury Station, my old station.
7. Recently they opened a station named for Dostoevsky, with beautiful gray and black marble murals of grim scenes from his novels.
8. Some beloved and hated dogs have apparently learned to navigate the metro: http://englishrussia.com/index.php/2009/04/07/smartest-dogs-moscow-stray-dogs/
9. The abandoned palace at Tsaritsyno has been completely rebuilt and is now a shiny tourist attraction.

"Remedies"

1. Although Wilco's "Passenger Side" (*AM*) was a close second, I have to go with "In Your Mind" by Built to Spill (*Ancient Melodies of the Future*) for the tone.
2. I can imagine Bryan playing either of those songs in his garage, though I feel Nick himself would be mostly a radio guy.
3. There aren't enough good stories set in Rockford, Illinois, though Richard Ford mentions it briefly in "Rock Springs," and Jennifer Egan's novel *Look at Me* really nails it. ▶

Trivia ***(continued)***

"Separate Kingdoms"

1. "Monkey Gone to Heaven" by the Pixies (*Doolittle*).
2. People ask me how they're supposed to read this story: one page at a time, one column at a time, or jumping back and forth. Read it however you like, really.
3. Initially I was interested in boredom and distraction in our lives and culture. I wondered what the practice of switching channels, literally and figuratively, every few minutes was doing to our reading habits. But it occurred to me that newspapers have long been designed with the understanding that a person will read one story for a little while, then maybe jump over to something that catches her eye in another column before or instead of turning the page to finish the first article. I wanted to write a story that embraced that practice, a story with some passages so dull (the drumming, the TV) that a reader would naturally hop across the gutter and read the other column for a while. I put in some bridges to encourage such jumps. But when I've heard from readers, I get the sense that not too many people read the story that way, which is OK too.
4. I learned how to play the drums in order to write this story.
5. For me, it's a companion story to "God of Fire." It was what I could write before I could write "God of Fire."

"I wondered what the practice of switching channels, literally and figuratively, every few minutes was doing to our reading habits."

Save the Stories

When people ask me why it's so hard to get a story collection published, I say there's one way they can make it easier: buy more story collections. Before they go extinct. If you're reading this, you're probably already on board, but anyway here are a few of my favorite story collections:

1. *This Way for the Gas, Ladies and Gentlemen* by Tadeusz Borowski (translated by Barbara Vedder). Borowski's narrator, Tadeusz, claims and blames himself for "a portion of the sad fame of Auschwitz" in the most raw and unflinching collection of stories I've ever read.
2. *Varieties of Disturbance* by Lydia Davis. These ruthlessly efficient little stories are blunt and astonishing, clever and intelligent, and subvert or simply ignore nearly every convention of storytelling.
3. *The Suitcase* by Sergei Dovlatov (translated by Antonina W. Bouis). I stole an image from this book and embedded it into mine as an homage to the man who made ludicrous, boozy, defeatist escapism seem like the only sensible response to the absurdities of Soviet and immigrant life. At the risk of oversimplifying and offending somebody or other, I'll just go ahead and call him the Soviet David Sedaris. Especially if it will bring his books back in print.
4. *The Coast of Chicago* by Stuart Dybek. Lyrical, sexy, funny, wise. One of our best living story writers, and one ▸

"At the risk of oversimplifying and offending somebody or other, I'll just go ahead and call him the Soviet David Sedaris. Especially if it will bring his books back in print."

who captures the Midwest as well as anyone can.

5. *Bad Behavior* by Mary Gaitskill. With courage, humor, and savage honesty, these stories make us look at things we would otherwise try not to see.
6. *Love and Obstacles* by Aleksandar Hemon. These stories are narrated with such confidence and seeming guilelessness that you feel you're reading someone's too-good-to-be-true private journal. And that someone is fascinating, funny and tough, and the stories he tells transport you to places you didn't even know existed.
7. *Reasons to Live* by Amy Hempel. Hempel has a talent for leaving things out of stories, juxtaposing the awful, the mundane, and the absurd in ways that delight and unsettle me.
8. *Jesus' Son* by Denis Johnson. His characters live moment by moment, unshackled from the tedious narrative burden of psychological motivation. If only we could all live and write like that, at least sometimes.
9. *No One Belongs Here More Than You* by Miranda July. These are love stories for the twenty-first century, unlike any that came before.
10. *At the Bottom of the River* by Jamaica Kincaid. Everybody keeps reading and rereading "Girl," and the rest of these strange and fearless stories have been sorely overlooked.
11. *Stories in the Worst Way* by Gary Lutz. These brief, dark, twisted glimpses into normal and abnormal lives will baffle and haunt you and make everything

"[Denis Johnson's] characters live moment by moment, unshackled from the tedious narrative burden of psychological motivation."

else you'll ever read seem horribly ordinary.

12. *Self-Help* by Lorrie Moore. There isn't room here to count the ways I admire Lorrie Moore. I'm a tremendous fan of all her collections, but this was the book that made me think maybe I could write stories, too.
13. *Civilwarland in Bad Decline* by George Saunders. If there's a more singular, bizarre, hilarious, and affecting voice in contemporary American fiction, I haven't found it.
14. *Street of Crocodiles* by Bruno Schulz (originally published as *Cinnamon Shops*; beautifully translated by Celina Wieniewska). Lyrical and luminous, with prose that knocks the breath from your body, these stories are like the dreams of an innocent but haunted, possibly deranged child.
15. *Ideas of Heaven* by Joan Silber. What these stories do with time, structure, and scope is so impressive and unique that you can't begin to predict where they might take you.

"If there's a more singular, bizarre, hilarious, and affecting voice in contemporary American fiction, I haven't found it."

Have You Read?
More by Valerie Laken

DREAM HOUSE

One of *Kirkus Reviews*'s Best Books of 2009 and winner of Anne Powers Award from the Council for Wisconsin Writers.

When Kate and Stuart buy a run-down historic house, they hope their grand renovation project can rescue their troubled marriage. Instead, they discover that years ago their home was the scene of a terrible crime—and the revelation tips the balance of their precarious union. A riveting debut novel about one troubled house—the site of a domestic drama that will forever change the lives of two families.

"The perfect haunted house story for these unnerving times. Laken divulges . . . information with the delicacy of a poet and the punch of an old hand at the suspense game. . . . Having assembled the plot machinery for a sturdy thriller, Laken does none of the expected things. Instead, she uses the framework to support an ambitious study of people in search of a home—'home' being a metaphor for the elusive something that defines and validates the self."

—*New York Times Book Review*

Don't miss the next book by your favorite author. Sign up now for AuthorTracker by visiting www.AuthorTracker.com.